Silent Night

A Book of Dreams Novel

Book Two

BRIDGETTE O'HARE

Silent Night
(A Book of Dreams Novel #2)
Second Edition
Copyright © 2015 by Bridgette O'Hare
Cloverhouse Publishing

ISBN-13: 9780986291555
ISBN-10: 0986291552

Cover design by EJR Designs

For my wonderful parents,

thank you for always believing in me.

Looking on darkness which the blind do see:
Save that my soul's imaginary sight
Presents thy shadow to my sightless view,
Which, like a jewel hung in ghastly night,
Makes black night beauteous and her old
face new.
Lo! thus, by day my limbs, by night my mind,
For thee, and for myself no quiet find.

Sonnet 27
~ William Shakespeare

Chapter One

Halle opened her eyes to a room void of light and the feeling she wasn't alone – a familiar feeling after dreams about her father. She squinted, searching the darkness to adjust. She glanced at the clock by her bed. Still too early to think about getting up on a Saturday. She sat up anyway. Sleeping soundly hadn't been the easiest thing to do in recent days. Every night, at some point, she found herself waking from a dream with that voice echoing in her head. His words haunting her. *"Do you have no sense of self-preservation, Miss Michaels? Are you not afraid? I can make every nightmare you've ever had seem like a lullaby."*

She was about to reach for the lamp,

needing a little light to chase away the shadows, when she thought she saw something move by the chair in the corner. She touched the lamp once for the dim setting and rubbed her eyes then looked again. Nothing. She shook her head. *Overactive imagination*.

She fumbled with the nightstand drawer until she pulled it open and found her newest journal, the pen still nesting between the pages from her last entry. She tapped the base of her lamp to add a little more light and began to write.

Another dream about Dad tonight. This one was kinda odd. Not that they aren't all odd considering I am dreaming about a man I don't really know. He showed up with a present in his hands. It was gorgeous...wrapped in beautiful iridescent white paper with a mound of swirling ribbon piled on top in a rainbow of colors. One of those presents that is almost too pretty to open. Almost.

I tore through the paper. When I opened the box it was the angel I already have, the one he bought me the day I was born. I remember looking at Dad confused and our conversation was something like this:

Me – I don't get it, Dad.

Dad – It's the first birthday present I ever gave you.

Me – Yeah, I get that.

Dad – Read the inscription.

Me – You mean the one on the bottom that I can't understand?

(Dad laughed)

Dad – Yes, Halle. That one.

(I read it aloud to him as best I could)

Me – Still don't understand it, Dad. (He just smiled at me)

Dad – You will. In due time, you will.

It was at this point that I looked down at the angel in my hands, turned it over and ran my fingers across the inscription. When I looked back up to tell Dad "thank you," he was gone.

Why do I keep having these freakazoid dreams?

Halle placed the pen back between the pages and closed the journal over it before slipping it back into the open drawer of the nightstand. She tapped the lamp base until it was dark in the room again and settled back into the heap of pillows behind her. There were still a few more hours of sleep to be had. After a few tosses back and forth she found a comfortable position and lay there thinking about her dad, what the inscription on the angel meant, and how dreams about him felt more real than life itself at times. She wondered if all the psychological types were right. Do dreams really always have meaning? If so, what do her dreams mean? And why do they keep invading reality?

"Uuhhh. Too many questions." She mumbled and twisted over again to face the bay window, pulling a pillow close the way she'd held her favorite bunny when she was little. A beam of light streaming through the window landed on the angel on her dresser. Not much help in clearing her mind of the questions. When the dog began barking incessantly outside, she began to doubt she'd get back to sleep at all.

"What is that blasted dog barking at now?" She grumbled and shoved the comforter away from her body before rolling out of bed. Prepared to shout a piece of her mind at the dog from the window, or at least give him something to distract from the target of his aggression, she plodded across the hardwood floor and plunked down on the window seat before opening the window. Her neighbor, Philip, was walking across his yard toward the dog. Whatever the dog was focusing on in the woods was clearly more pressing than Philip's presence. He didn't seem to be curtailing the dog's barking at all.

Halle had always avoided going near those woods. As a girl, they scared her. Many times she swore she'd seen things in them. Sometimes she was sure she had seen people watching her from behind trees. The woods border with the national forest and wrap around two-thirds of the lake then stretches into the mountains and on toward Ashville. Halle had always known it wouldn't be hard to get lost in them.

Aedan traded the comfy chair for a window seat beside Halle. He had already learned that Ruman wasn't one to bark for no reason and he had proven his guard dog skills more than once. His persistent barking was an alarm as far as Aedan was concerned. He watched Philip stare into the trees for a while and then kneel down beside the dog as though he were talking to him. For several minutes, both Philip and Ruman remained in that position searching the woods. Aedan did a scan of the area himself. There were Hellions, but he wasn't sure how many. He only caught two as they retreated out of detection range.

Philip appeared to say something into the dog's ear before standing and heading back to the house. The dog followed, seeming to keep a watchful eye on the wooded area as he retreated slowly. When they reached the porch, Philip glanced toward Halle's window before disappearing into the house. Halle wasn't sure if he'd seen her or not. She watched for a moment while the dog situated himself on the porch facing the woods like a guardian.

"Crazy dog." Halle said with a half-smile.

"I kinda like the dog." Aedan muttered under his breath, still scanning the woods for stragglers.

Halle paused and looked around. The voice was quiet and calming, not deafening like the ones she'd been hearing recently.

Aedan turned to find Halle staring right at him. He immediately hoped he hadn't materialized again without warning. Not that he'd know the warning signs if there were any. Had Halle been any typical charge, he'd have expected her to scream bloody murder if she saw a man sitting in her bedroom across from her at three in the morning. He'd already learned she wasn't typical. A typical mortal wouldn't have headed into a room a burglar might be in or back toward a gas truck about to explode.

A moment later, Halle was moving back to her bed and Aedan felt as though he could breathe again.

The warrior in him wanted to track down the Hellions he'd sensed in the woods and beat the information he wanted out of them. Why were they there? Who sent them and what were they after? They couldn't possibly already know about the book in Halle's possession. He had only let her out of his sight for the short time he spoke with Darius. If they did already know about it, the question was how?

It unnerved him knowing any other time he'd have already been on their trail. How could she confuse and infuriate him so and still elicit his protective instinct so strongly? He wasn't even sure she needed protection at this point. Part of him questioned where her allegiance would fall if faced with the choice. Regardless of his personal conflict, Philip needed to know what he had sensed in the woods. He opened a line of communication and told him what he knew. Short and to the point.

Aedan spent the remainder of the night watching Halle and fighting his internal battles.

Chapter Two

Saturday mornings were Halle's day to sleep in, but that didn't seem to be possible. She'd been awake since before the sun invaded her room. After precisely thirty-seven minutes of tossing and turning, and approximately fifteen times of looking at the time on the clock; she dragged herself from bed, took a shower, and put away the stack of folded laundry Lana had left her the night before. So far, it qualified as the most productive Saturday since she had to clean out her closet.

With the last pair of jeans put away, Halle picked up the wooden box she'd received the day before, snagged her laptop from her desk, and headed back to her bed. With the box situated beside her and the computer in her lap, her fingers tapped away to unlock her laptop. Just as she was about to start what she was sure would be a futile search for anything she could find on the book Toby had sent her, her messenger window popped onscreen.

tOBI-Wan: Hey Kiddo! You awake yet?
A smile formed and she shook her head.
DreamGirl: Hard to believe, but yes.
tOBI-Wan: I got your message. Sorry I wasn't around. Had a 911 at the dig site.
DreamGirl: It's ok. I didn't die of curiosity. It was a close call though. ☺
tOBI-Wan: LOL. Good to know you survived. Skype? I know you're dying to ask me 100 ???s
DreamGirl: Yes. Yes I am.

Before she could close the IM, he was calling.

"Good morning, sunshine." Toby was chipper. Of course, it was six hours later there.

Halle smiled. "Well, it's morning. I'll let you know how good later."

Toby laughed. "You're up kinda early. And by kinda early I mean, are you feelin' okay kinda early."

"Not by choice, I assure you."

"What has you all insomniatic this

morning?"

"I think the appropriate question would be what doesn't?"

Toby arched an eyebrow. "Have things been ok for you lately, Hal?"

How do you explain that your dreams and reality are colliding, you're hearing voices, and not so sure you aren't losing your mind? "Yeah, Uncle T. Things are fine." You don't.

"So, I take it you got your birthday present." He smiled mischievously.

"Yes!"

"And you have questions."

"I do."

"What do you want to know?"

Halle tilted her head a little, contemplating what to ask first. "Umm. Everything? But first, where's the key?"

"Key?"

"Yeah. It's locked." Halle opened the box and grabbed the book while she finished her sentence. "It needs a – whoa." The book fell open in her hands. She maneuvered to catch it.

"You were saying?" Toby smirked.

Halle pursed her lips and eyed the book lying open in her lap. "It was locked yesterday. I'm sure of it. I even contemplated going all cat burglar on it with a screwdriver."

Toby laughed again. "Are you sure you

didn't? I mean, it's open now."

She studied the lock again. Still no lever or latch that she missed before. "Odd. I dunno." She turned a few pages. They were blank. "Was it locked when you sent it?"

"Well, yes. But to be honest, I kind of thought you might have a key."

Halle stopped studying the lock and looked at Toby. "Why would you think that?"

"You're dad had a book that looked just like that one. That's why I gave it to you. Thought maybe it was a set of some kind that might have been separated through the years."

Halle was intrigued. "I've never seen a book anything like this. Ever."

"Maybe your mom knows where it is. I remember seeing it in your dad's office a lot. I figured there must be a key to it since sometimes it was open and sometimes it was locked."

She looked at the book and flipped another page. She was about to keep flipping when she noticed that one had a line written across the bottom. "Hey, Uncle T. This page has writing." She studied the markings for a moment. "What language is this?" Halle held the book up to the webcam for him to see.

"Bring it a little closer to the camera." He studied it a moment. "Interesting."

Halle pulled the book down and moved closer to the webcam. "What's interesting?"

"There are two different languages there."

She pulled the book back to her lap so she could look at them.

"The top phrase is Latin. The bottom is Hebrew. Strange."

"What's strange about that?" Halle turned a few more pages, looking for more writing.

"You just don't see those two languages together like that. At least, I never have."

"Well, where'd you find the book?"

He paused long enough that Halle looked up from her word search through the book.

"Kind of a funny story. It found me."

"Do tell."

"It showed up at my office inside a box of items someone sent me from an estate sale. The wooden box was stuck shut so they probably thought it was worthless. When I finally got the thing open and saw it was just like your dad's book, I thought you'd want it."

"I'm going to have to ask Mom about Dad's book. I've never seen it."

"I know she has a few boxes of Noah's things still in the attic. Maybe it's there."

Halle beamed. "I'll ask her. Can you translate these phrases for me?"

"Sure, take a pic and email it to me."

Halle's mouth curved slightly. "All of them?"

"What do you mean *all* of them?" Toby looked worried. He'd seen that look before.

"I don't know exactly how many there are, but I've found four so far just flipping through." Her smile grew into a grin.

"Yeah. Might be a day or two before I have time to get to them, but send them all to me."

"Sweet. Will do. Have you talked to Mom lately?"

"Earlier this week. Why? Everything okay?" Concern washed over his face.

"Yeah, everything's fine. Typical week in the Michaels' household I guess. I was just wondering."

"Umm. Okay. Well, I have to get back to work. Don't get weekends off here if I want to get back to the states any time soon."

"Alrighty. Thank you for the book. It's very cool. I love it." Her smile lit up.

"I knew you would. I'll talk to you on Friday, Princess."

"Friday?" She narrowed her eyes in uncertainty.

"Yeah. Friday. Your birthday."

Her eyes flashed big. "Oh. Right. Duh."

Toby laughed and shook his head. "Love ya, kiddo. Talk to you soon."

"Love you too, Uncle T. Thanks again. Bye."

She blew him a kiss as he signed off and then she sat there, going through the pages. It was a lot to process. She didn't want to wait two days to know what the phrases said. She'd counted seven in all, randomly scattered throughout the book, but all in the same place on each page. There didn't seem to be a pattern to how they were distributed.

After taking pics of the phrases with her phone and sending them to Toby, she spent the next hour with an online Latin translator, attempting to decipher the phrases into English. No doubt butchering them in the process, but trying to get some idea of what they meant. Again, patience was not her strong suit.

She was about to close out the translation site when a light bulb moment hit. The phrase on the base of the angel from her dad. Toby told her once it was Latin. She was fairly certain he had also told her what it said, but she couldn't seem to remember what that was. She jumped up and grabbed it, then bounced back onto her bed and typed the phrase into the search box.

Fallaces sunt rerum species. Somnis vide infra claustrum.

She was sure it wasn't an exact translation, but it was interesting all the same.

Appearances deceive. Inside your dreams is key.

Lana knocked on her door and pushed it open as she was reading. "I got you something." She held a new cell phone in her hand and waved it subtly back and forth.

"Ohhh, Mom, you're the best!" Halle jumped up and hurried to her, throwing her arms around her neck.

"I know." Lana teased. "Steve had the guys at the crime lab extract all your files and contacts from your melted phone and put them on a card so you didn't lose any of your photos or whatever. It's all there on the new phone."

Halle grinned and bounced a little as she took the phone from Lana. "That is so awesome. Thank you!"

"You're welcome, sweetheart. Couldn't really have you going on a date tonight with no way to call home if he's a jerk, now could I?"

The date. Crap. She'd forgotten. Brandt Lucas. High school heart-throb who didn't take *no* for an answer. She sighed. "I actually forgot." She thudded her head to rest against the wall. "Wait, how'd you know I have a date?" Without losing contact with the wall, she pivoted her head and squinted her eyes at Lana.

"I have my ways."

Halle raised an inquisitive eyebrow. "Jenna?"

"Jenna."

"Big mouth." Halle mumbled.

"When were you going to tell me?" Lana leaned against the doorframe and crossed her arms.

"I'm sure I would have told you last night, but with all the excitement, I seriously kinda forgot until just now." She glanced at the clock. "He's picking me up at six."

"Can't say I'm too sure what it says about the guy if you forgot." Lana chuckled.

"I know, but I have eight hours until he gets here. It's all good."

Lana smiled and shook her head. "Well, Jenna said she'd be here at one to help you find something to wear. Oh, and you might want to check that phone. It's been buzzin' since they turned it on at the store." Lana turned and headed for the stairs.

"Hey, Mom."

"Yeah?"

"Do you know anything about this book?" Halle walked to her bed and picked the book up.

Lana's eyes grew wide. She tried to mask it, but Halle knew her mother much too well. She walked back into Halle's room and took the book from Halle, ran her hand softly over it and opened the cover. "Where did you get this?" Astonishment laced her words.

"Uncle T sent it to me for my birthday. It was on the doorstep when I got home yesterday. He said Dad had one like it."

Lana nodded her head, blinking heavily. "He did. But I haven't seen it since before he died." She caressed the pages as she turned them. "Wow." She whispered.

"What?"

"It looks just like it. Only —" Lana paused as she turned page after page.

"Only what?"

"Well, your father used to write in his, in Hebrew none the less. He always said a book that old should be written in with a language just as old." Her smile lit up as she remembered.

"What did he write in it?" Halle's curiosity grew.

Lana closed the book and handed it back to Halle. "I have no idea." A quiet laugh escaped. "I know two languages. Hebrew isn't one of them."

"Uncle T said there might have been a key to this thing. Do you know anything about that?" Halle pointed out the locking mechanism.

"No. I don't remember finding anything like that in your dad's desk when we were putting his things away. Of course, Toby did most of that about six months after your dad died. I couldn't bring myself to go through any of it."

"Do you think it might be in one of the boxes in the attic?"

Lana considered the possibility. "Could be. Ask Toby if he remembers packing it. I know I didn't."

It was obvious she still missed Noah.

"Sorry, Mom."

"Nothing to apologize for dear." She stroked her hand across Halle's tousled hair and leaned in to kiss her forehead. "I made some apple streusel muffins this morning if you want one and there's fruit in the fridge. I have to run to the office for a few, but I'll be back well before your date arrives." She winked at Halle. "Call me if you need me."

"Thanks, Mom. Love you."

"Love you, too. See you in a bit." Lana closed Halle's door as she left, leaving Halle alone with the book and more questions. She contemplated an all-out run for the attic to rummage through the boxes from Noah's office, until her new phone began to buzz.

"Hello?"

"Welcome back to the grid." Jenna's voice chimed through the line.

"Yeah. Thanks. I think."

"Whatcha doin'?"

"You wouldn't believe me if I told you." Halle glanced down at the book under her arm.

"Try me."

Halle gave Jenna the highlights of the events from the time she received the book the afternoon before to the recent conversation with Lana. By the time she was done, the doorbell was ringing.

"Hey Jen, let me call you back. Someone's at the door."

"Yeah, I know. It's me. Come let me in."

Halle laid the book on the bed, and bounced down the stairs to the mudroom. Jenna had her face pressed to the glass as if she was looking in a shoe store window waiting for the owner to open the door on a half-price sale. Halle shook her head and unlocked the door.

"You are a disturbed individual. You know that, right?" Halle still had the phone to her ear.

"Says the girl who tried to run toward an exploding gas truck yesterday." Jenna smiled and walked past her into the kitchen. "I smell baking."

Halle shoved the phone into the pocket of her jeans and followed Jenna. "You get the milk. I'll get the muffins."

"It's like you can read my mind. This is precisely why we're best friends."

"My mom's baking?" Halle laughed.

"Well, that doesn't hurt either." Jenna poured the milk. "So, have you decided what you're wearing tonight?"

Halle made a grunting sound.

"That would be a no." Jenna sat the glasses of milk on the counter and hopped on a barstool.

Halle took a seat beside her with the muffins and fruit already on the counter. Jenna eyed the fruit a moment and pushed the bowl out of the way to reach for a muffin.

"We'll head up and raid your closet after this." Jenna bit into a muffin and darted her eyes upward. "So good." It barely came out audible.

Halle smiled and bit into a strawberry.

Once Jenna could make comprehendible words again, she spoke. "So what's the deal with this book Toby sent you?"

"Not sure yet. I was thinking of tearing through a few boxes in the attic to see if Dad's matching book might be up there. Wanna help?"

Jenna nodded. "Sure." She took her last bite and finished off her milk.

Halle put the fruit back in the fridge and they headed to the attic.

Hours later, and more conversation than Halle had intended, Jenna knew about some of Halle's crazy dreams – including the one that had them both running for their lives from an exploding truck just 24 hours earlier – and every box in the attic marked with Noah's name had been ransacked. No book to be found. No key. No secrets.

While attempting to put the boxes back into some semblance of order, Jenna bumped into a stack and sent the top box tumbling to the floor. The lid flew one way and the box another.

"Hey, Hal." Jenna called from the opposite end of the attic. "Halle. Come see this."

When Halle rounded a stack of boxes, she saw Jenna with a striking, deep red ball gown held close to her chest.

"I think I know what you're wearing to the masquerade ball." Jenna's eyes were lit up. "How gorgeous is this?"

"Holy – where'd you find that?" Halle walked over and touched the beadwork around the waist. Simple, elegant beadwork.

Jenna smiled. "I sort of knocked it over. It's a gift. You're welcome."

"I wonder where it came from." Halle picked up the box from the floor. Even the velvet-lined box was exquisite.

Jenna was searching through the lining of the dress. "There's no tag. Wait. Here's something."

"What?" Halle leaned in to get a better look.

"Here." Jenna pointed to a hand-sewn label. "This dress is seriously vintage. It's crazy heavy too."

Jenna handed it to Halle.

"Wow."

"Wow is right." Jenna eyed the dress more carefully from her new angle. "This is a hand-sewn masterpiece. I think you should try it on."

Just then, Halle's phone buzzed in her pocket. She wrapped one arm around the waist of the dress and pulled her phone out with the other.

"Text from Brandt." She relayed to Jenna. "Holy crap! Do you know what time it is?" Panic spread across her face. "I have like two hours to get ready and I have no idea what I'm going to wear."

"Breathe." Jenna reached over calmly and took the dress from Halle. "We will play Halloween dress up with this later. Right now let's go focus on dress up for tonight." She made easy work of arranging the dress back in its box. It was almost as though she had done it before.

Halle put the lid in place and followed Jenna to the stairs, switching off the light as she pulled the attic door closed.

Chapter Three

Having the capability to sense Hellions in the area made Aedan a little more at ease with the idea of staying near Halle without being so close to her. Having Ruman around as an alarm system didn't hurt either. Especially since being close to her was proving to be more and more uncomfortable. The term painful was more accurate.

That detail had Aedan spending the afternoon hiding out behind the safe house practicing the newest weapons in his arsenal. He was feeling confident in his ability to transform at will back and forth into physical form. A confidence that was tested when a familiar voice called out to him.

"Think fast."

He turned just in time to reach his hand in front of his face and catch the hard, red ball.

"That's a new trick." Sapphira smiled as she approached. "Might come in handy."

"Or cause more problems." Aedan tossed the ball back to her.

"Does Darius know about this?" She made her way to one of the patio chairs situated near the dock and sat down. Aedan took a seat that allowed him a good view on the house next door.

"He knows. Who do you think gave me the pointers on learning to control it?"

"Hmmph." Sapphira gave him a contemplative stare.

"What's that look for?"

"Just wondering about something." She smiled playfully.

Aedan knew that smile. It never meant anything good for him. "I'm a little afraid to ask."

"You don't have to ask. I'm going to say it anyway." She paused and tilted her head in a way Aedan knew was purely for dramatic effect. "You know something about her, don't you? Something you aren't sharing."

Aedan stared at the window to Halle's room, calculating what he should say. There was a lot he wasn't telling Sapphira, or anyone for that matter. They had no idea how much contact he'd had with Halle in dream realms, how painful her touch was to him, his doubts about her mortality, or the electrical charge that surged through him just being near her and pulled him closer to her at the same time. Until he figured some things out, it was best to keep those things under wraps.

"She has a date tonight." He didn't know what else to say and he hoped that would derail the train of inquisition Sapphira was about to run him over with.

Sapphira laughed. "Really? That's what has you so worked up?"

Aedan darted a glare in her direction. "Worked up? I'm not worked up."

She rolled her eyes at him. "Ok. If you say so." She tried to hide the smile that crept across her lips. "So who is her date with?"

"Some punk named Brandt Lucas. Know anything about him?"

She bobbed her head a little. "He goes to school with her. He's popular. All the girls follow him around like lost puppies. And you have to admit, the kid is pretty good looking. That's about all I have. What do you know about him?" Sapphira couldn't wait to hear his answer. She already knew how Aedan felt about him by the tone he used saying his name.

"Not enough." His eyes narrowed as he focused intently on the car pulling into Halle's driveway. "I know he's punctual." The last word was emphasized.

Sapphira turned to see Brandt strolling up the walkway to Halle's front door.

The sound of the doorbell was followed immediately by the padded sound of hurried footsteps as Jenna ran to the window. "Yep. It's him. You ready?" A sly grin played on her lips.

"If I say no, do I still have to go?"

Jenna puckered her lips together in a mock thinking gesture before a blunt, "Yes."

"Then I guess it doesn't matter, does it?"

"C'mon. It'll be fun." Jenna stepped between Halle and the mirror, adjusted Halle's necklace and touched up a flyaway sprig of hair. "You. Look. Amazing."

Halle sucked in a deep breath and blew it out heavily. "Why am I nervous?"

"Ummm, because you haven't been on a date in like two years?"

She opened her mouth to say something and bobbed her head in agreement before the word spilled out, "Yeah."

Lana appeared in the doorway. "He's cuuute, and charming. Let's not make him wait too long, ok?" She smiled.

"Too late to chicken out now." Jenna

scoffed. "He's already met your mom."

Halle ran a streak of lip gloss over her bottom lip and blended it.

"Let's get you to your date." Jenna grabbed Halle's purse and handed it to her before walking into the hallway. When Halle didn't budge, Jenna gave her a what-are-you-waiting-for look.

After another deep breath, Halle picked up her jacket from the bed and headed for the stairs. Her phone buzzed as she was about to take the first step down. A quick glance showed a text from Matt. Jenna stopped halfway down. Halle mouthed, "It's from Matt."

Jenna snagged the phone from Halle's hand and read it.

Why is Brandt's car in your driveway?

Jenna mouthed back, "Oh crap." And nodded in a manner suggesting Halle get out of the house as quickly as possible.

Brandt was standing in the living room, intently looking at books on a shelf when Halle walked in. He almost seemed startled when she said hello.

"Wow. You look . . . wow." Brandt smiled, tongue-tied.

Halle was immediately glad Jenna had talked her into the dressier outfit. While Brandt always looked good at school in jeans and a polo, they clearly didn't do him justice compared to the flat front black khakis and tailored button down shirt he was wearing. His hair had its usual perfectly spiked, tousled style. Halle had to admit, he cleaned up nicely.

He just stood there smiling at Halle until Jenna interrupted the silence.

"So, Brandt, where are you taking our fair Halle?"

"We have dinner reservations at a new Italian restaurant on the south side of the lake."

Jenna feigned surprise. "What a coincidence. Halle loves Italian food. Right, Hal?"

"As a matter of fact, I do." Halle suddenly had the suspicion that Jenna had a little something to do with that coincidence.

Brandt glanced at his watch. "We should probably get going. Our reservations are in an hour. It's a forty-five minute drive."

They walked into the kitchen where Lana was reading some mail. Brandt stopped and spoke to her.

"It was a pleasure to meet you Mrs. Michaels. What time would you like for me to have Halle home?" Jenna was standing behind Brandt mouthing something to Lana she couldn't quite make out.

Lana tried to suppress her amusement at Jenna. "That's very polite of you to ask, Brandt. I think any time before midnight will be fine."

"Yes ma'am." Brandt nodded and turned to Jenna who quickly refrained from her gesturing. "See ya later, Jenna."

Jenna just waved from her frozen position.

Halle gave her mother a kiss on the cheek and said goodbye to her and Jenna. Brandt followed her outside.

Sapphira had cloaked her physical form and was standing with Aedan by the shiny black sports car when Halle and Brandt emerged from the house. Aedan's attention immediately focused on Halle.

If it was possible, she looked less and less human to Aedan every time he looked at her.

"Am I the only one who sees that?" It was said under his breath.

"Sees what?" Sapphira had no idea what Aedan was talking about.

"Does she look...I don't know...human to you?"

"Umm, yes. How else would she look? And why wouldn't she?" Sapphira stared at Halle as she moved toward them, looking for anything unusual that may have triggered Aedan's comment.

"She's just . . . I've never . . ." Aedan had no idea how to explain what he saw when he looked at Halle. "Nevermind. I'm sure it's just my imagination."

Sapphira smiled knowingly. "She's special, Aedan. I get it."

"She's *something*. That's for sure. The question is what?" Aedan watched as Brandt opened Halle's door for her.

Sapphira chuckled. "He's been coached well." She motioned for Aedan to follow her. "C'mon. You can ride with me."

Aedan stood there a moment.

"Well, either you ride with me and we can follow them in case she needs us, or you can ride with them." Sapphira waited for his response.

"Get the keys."

"That's what I thought."

Halle couldn't get over the atmosphere at the restaurant as she followed the hostess through the main dining room. It was spacious, but still had a cozy, romantic quality. Brandt chose well. She didn't realize how well until they entered a smaller room in the back of the restaurant. Four tables sat spaced much further apart than those in the main dining room. A more private setting. When the hostess seated them at a table by the large glass windows, Halle caught a glimpse of the view. She could see the Charlotte skyline shadowed against the dusky sky on the horizon. Brandt helped her with her chair and then sat across from her. The hostess disappeared, leaving them alone in the room.

The lights of Charlotte glimmering in the distance had Halle transfixed on the horizon. "That is quite the view."

"Yes it is." Brandt replied, but he wasn't looking at the skyline. Heat caressed her cheeks when she realized what he meant. *Smooth*, she thought. The question certainly wasn't if he was smooth though, it was if he was sincere. Sometimes his words and actions seemed a little too rehearsed. Almost perfect.

For a while, they sat in silence as Halle pretended to mull over the menu even though she had decided what she wanted after the first pass. Once the waiter had taken their order, Halle stared at the view. Brandt stared at Halle.

He broke the silence. "You really do look amazing."

The blush on her cheeks was proof she wasn't used to compliments. She hadn't put herself in a situation to be complimented since Cam, her last boyfriend. "Thanks. You don't look too shabby yourself."

By the time their food arrived they had both loosened up a little. Brandt even admitted he had made a list of conversation topics in case of awkward silence. They went down the list and talked about music and movies until the conversation took a turn of its own. When dessert arrived, they were on the subject of super hero powers.

"If you could have any super power, what would it be?" Halle smiled as she took a bite of her cheesecake and waited for an answer.

"Hmm. That's a tough one." Brandt thought for a moment. "I think I'd like to be able to hear what other people are thinking. You know, read minds."

Halle almost choked.

"Are you ok?" Brandt asked.

Halle nodded, finished choking down the cheesecake, and took a sip of water. "Yeah, just went down wrong. Sorry."

A mischievous grin spread across his face. "I know mouth to mouth if you need it."

"Cute." She smiled back.

"Thanks, I try. So, you want to tell me what your super power would be? Or are you going to get all choked up on me again? Because, I'll be happy to help with CPR if necessary." He winked.

Halle tilted her head and eyed him curiously. "Are you certified?"

He laughed. "Would it help my case if I were?"

"I'll let you know." She took another sip of water to break the conversation. "So. You want to know what super power I'd have or not?"

"Well, since I don't have the one I want, you're going to have to tell me." He leaned back in his seat. Clearly more relaxed than when they arrived.

"I think I'd like to be able to take your powers."

"You want to take my mind reading?"

"Not just yours. Anyone's. Whatever your power is, I could take it and use it as my own."

"Ohhhh. Sneaky. And brilliant really. You came up with that just now, did you?" He flashed a confident grin.

"Well, not really. I actually had a dream once that I could do just that. You wouldn't believe how powerful I could be if superpowers really existed." She gave her most ominous glare.

They both laughed. She knew that was one dream that would never snake its way into her reality. People with superpowers just didn't exist.

Aedan had insisted on staying away from Halle's date.

"But I want to see how it's going." Sapphira

insisted. "We've been sitting on this patio for over an hour. Now, I know you don't seem to grasp the time concept, but after spending so much of it in mortal form, I'm starting to catch on."

"Yeah, well, I don't really care how it's going. I can see her through the window from here. She's safe. That's all I need to know." Aedan focused his gaze on Halle. It wasn't hard to. She was like a beacon. The faint glow he noticed the first time he saw her seemed to intensify daily. How Sapphira, or anyone else, didn't notice it was a mystery. "Besides, you've been in there twice already."

"Yeah, and all I got was a conversation about CPR and super powers. Although, he did offer to give her mouth to mouth." Sapphira watched Aedan's reaction closely.

He took a deep breath and resituated himself in his chair, obviously irritated.

"Uhhh, Aedan."

"What?" His tone was sharp.

"Good thing no one else is out here. You might want to practice a little more." Sapphira smirked a little.

He had transferred to mortal form and had a death grip on the arm of the chair.

A slight smile tugged at her lips. "Emotional transformations are the hardest to control."

He loosed his grip on the chair. "There's nothing emotional going on. You know me. I don't do emotion."

Her smile faded. She remembered a time when he hadn't guarded himself so relentlessly. "You can't hide from the shadows inside you forever, Aedan. What good is your heart if you can't open it and let yourself out?"

He wasn't about to respond to Sapphira's observation. No good would come of it. His focus remained on Halle. For a moment he was certain their stares locked. Then she stood.

"They're leaving."

Sapphira glanced over her shoulder to see Halle and Brandt disappearing from view. "I guess that's our cue."

Brandt pulled into Halle's driveway at 11:43 pm. Aedan and Sapphira arrived at the safe house minutes later. Sapphira pressed the button to close the garage door and exited the car.

"Being stealthy as a mortal is not easy." She tossed the keys in to the front seat where she always left them.

Aedan silently agreed. "Don't you want to see how her date ends?" He tried to keep his tone void of any inflection, but there was a hint of sarcasm laced in.

Sapphira shot him a look of curiosity. "Of course I do. But isn't it your job to watch her now?"

"Yes. The difference is I don't really care to see how her date ends." His expression remained steady.

She bit back a satisfied smirk. "You may not care to see, but you do care."

Aedan blew out a frustrated breath. "Just go. I'm going to find Darius." He traced out before she had a chance to say another word.

When Sapphira arrived at Halle's, Jenna and Lana were trying to watch undetected through the window as Halle and Brandt stood on the porch saying their goodnights.

For the first time all evening Halle watched Brandt stumble over his words. "I . . . I, uh, really had a great time, Halle."

"Yeah. It was fun. Thank you for dinner and the movie." She smiled shyly. This was the part of the date she had been dreading. The awkward moment when you don't know what to expect. Kiss goodnight or not?

Brandt moved a step closer to her, his voice softened. "I would really like to take you out again, if you'll let me."

When Halle looked up to meet his stare, a flash from a dream broke through. She blinked a few times to clear the image from her mind.

"Well?" Brandt asked again, "Next weekend? Will you let me?"

She smiled. Trying to buy some time before answering. She had no idea how she wanted to answer. "I'm pretty booked next weekend."

"Oh." His expression darkened.

"It's my birthday. Kinda already have plans Friday and Saturday."

"Ohhh." He seemed a little relieved. "So it's not personal then? I didn't completely bore you to tears tonight?"

She laughed quietly. "No. I honestly did have a nice time and you've been a complete gentleman."

"Great." He flashed the confident smile he was known for. "So does that mean you'll go out with me again when your schedule isn't full?"

"I'll think about it." Her smile encouraged him.

"I'll be thinking about it too, then. Every day until you agree to go out with me again. And in keeping with the gentlemanly roll I'm on, I will say good night, promise to call you and leave you with this." He locked his eyes with hers and leaned in slowly. Every nerve in Halle's body stood on edge until his lips rested on her cheek. "Goodnight, Halle." He whispered in her ear before pulling back.

"Goodnight, Brandt." She watched him

stroll back to his car before she turned to open the front door.

She barely had the door shut behind her when Jenna barreled in from the living room.

"Oh. My. Great. He didn't even kiss you kiss you."

Halle's mouth gaped open in disbelief. "Were you watching?"

"Oh, c'mon. Do not even tell me that surprises you."

Halle nodded her head to the side with partial eye roll. "Ok. It really doesn't surprise me, but seriously?"

"Yes. I was watching. And we both want to know all about the date. C'mon. Your mom's in the living room." Jenna all but dragged Halle through the kitchen.

After listening to the rundown from the evening, Jenna announced she had to get home.

"I'll walk you out." Halle followed Jenna to the door and they stepped outside.

"Ok, Hal. Spill it. What gives?"

"About?"

"Brandt. What else? Why are you not making plans for another date already? Didn't you have a good time?"

Halle paused. Jenna knew what it meant when Halle paused. Uncertainty.

"I did have a good time – "

Jenna cut her off. "But. There's always a but."

"I just don't know if I'll go out with him again, is all."

"You're not telling me something Halle Michaels. What is it?"

Halle shrugged.

Jenna prodded for a minute and then it dawned on her.

"Ohhhhhh. I know what it is." Jenna's eyes widened.

"Really? You think you can just read my mind, huh?"

"You're waiting for that dream, aren't you?"

"What dream? I only have twelve journals full of them."

"Chair guy from the park. What was his name?" Jenna was trying to remember.

"Aedan." Halle said softly. "And no. That isn't it."

Jenna's expression faded to serious. "Hal, those are just dreams. You've had what, two or three smash into your reality? The odds are against it. Chair guy isn't your reality. Brandt is real."

"Jen, you know his reputation as well as I do. You know he's probably just playin' some game with me."

After a deep breath, Jenna looked Halle

square in the eyes with as much seriousness as Halle had seen in a while. "What I know is that you don't believe love happens anymore. But it does. It can. You have to let your guard down again sometime, Hal, and it shouldn't be just in dreams."

Halle nodded. "I know. But, if what I feel in those dreams is how I should feel in reality, then Brandt really missed the target."

"Give the guy a chance. I'd guess he's way more your type than dreamy chair guy is." Jenna winked. "Think about it. I'll talk to you tomorrow. We need to smooth out birthday plans for next weekend."

"Okay." Halle hugged Jenna. "Thanks, Jen. Goodnight."

"That's what I'm here for. 'Night."

Halle watched Jenna until she disappeared into her house down the street.

Chapter Four

Aedan stood and watched as Halle absorbed and returned the blunt force of a bolt of energy fired at her by an immortal, one Aedan didn't recognize. He tried to remind himself that every dream she had wasn't necessarily a premonition. Sometimes, they were just dreams. But watching her revert the blue missile-like force back at her attacker felt a little too familiar. There were just too many little things adding up for any of them to be coincidences anymore.

Halle's dream only fueled Aedan's belief that she wasn't at all what everyone thought she was. How could she have such vivid and accurate knowledge of a Guardian weapon? It wasn't like the half-guesses he had seen the weapon portrayed as on television or in movies. Halle's version was spot on. And she knew how to not only use it, but use it against an immortal.

Energy manipulation was only one ability in the arsenal Guardians and Hellions alike could pull from. It may have only been a dream, but Aedan had seen what Halle's dreams could do. Add in the book which had showed up on her doorstep that clearly had a locking device forged by the Sanhedrin guarding its pages, and the otherworldly glow she emitted, and Aedan was left wondering what other abilities and Guardian secrets this girl was aware of?

He made a mental list of questions to ask as he waited for Jess and Darius by the dock. Surely Darius had some idea as to what was going on.

Jess arrived first. "So, you want to fill me in on all the fun you've had while I was gone?"

Aedan wasn't in the mood to give details of everything Jess had missed. "I don't know what assignment you've been on, but I don't recall there being any fun around here."

Jess grinned. "There's always fun to be had. You just have to know where to find it."

Aedan didn't know how Jess had managed to keep a positive outlook after everything he had witnessed right alongside Aedan throughout the centuries. "Okay then, why don't you tell me what fun you've been getting into."

Jess fell back into the hammock and laced

his fingers behind his head. "Well, remember that book Apollo and crew were talking about?"

"I remember."

"Seems they think it has information in it that will get them something they've been after for centuries."

"And just what might that be?" Aedan felt his nerves stand on end.

"Payback."

"Did you find out what's in this book anyway?"

"Not a clue. I was hoping Darius might have some idea."

"He doesn't." Darius' commanding voice sliced into the conversation.

Jess swung his feet to the side of the hammock and sat up. "Well, if we don't know what we're after or why, how are we supposed to come up with a game plan?"

Darius stood silent for a moment. "Jess, just tell me what you do know about the book. Everything you learned. Everything you heard."

Jess went on to give the description Apollo had given to his search party and explain that this was no small time operation. "I haven't seen them rally the troops like this in ages."

Aedan gave Darius a concerned glare. "You know what I'm thinking, don't you?"

Darius nodded.

"Well, I don't. Someone want to fill me in?" Jess stood.

"We know it isn't Halle's book. Her's doesn't have anything written in it." Aedan continued. "That only leaves –"

Darius finished the thought. "Noah's."

"This isn't good, Darius. If they find out Halle has that book they're going to think. . . "

"I know."

"That must have been what they were looking for in Halle's house the first night I was here." Aedan took a seat.

"Would someone please tell me what is going on?" Jess stepped closer to the conversation. "Halle has the book?"

Aedan ran his hand through his hair. "The book you described. Halle has one."

Jess could have been knocked over with a feather. "What do you mean *one*? That implies there are others."

"That's because there apparently is another."

"Darius? How can there be two of them?" Jess asked.

"I don't know." Darius replied. "But Halle received one a couple of days ago that looks exactly like one Noah had. Like the one you described. He used to write in it. That has to be the one they're after."

"What exactly did he write in this book?" The sinking feeling in Aedan's core was plummeting. Fast. "And where is the book now?"

"I don't know. Noah was never part of my assignment."

Jess asked what Aedan was thinking. "Whose assignment was Noah part of?"

Darius' expression betrayed him before he ever spoke. His eyes grew distant. "I'm not at liberty to say. But I'll find out what I can."

"What do you mean you can't say?" Aedan demanded. "I need to know what I'm dealing with here. How can I protect her if I don't know what I'm protecting her from?"

"Aedan, there are just some things that I can't tell you. Not now. Just don't let her out of your sight. Do whatever you have to do. You have full permission to pull out all the stops. You especially can't let Apollo or Keros near her. If my instincts are right, she's our best chance to find Noah's book." Darius turned to leave, but Aedan wasn't satisfied.

"Darius —"

"Aedan, I'll tell you what I can, as soon as I can. You have to let this go for now and trust me." Darius traced out before Jess or Aedan had a chance to argue.

"There's only one reason Darius would keep

that from us, isn't there?" Jess paced a few steps and stopped.

"That would be my guess."

"Do you really think this book is what Apollo and Keros think it is? I mean, was Noah that high on the food chain?"

Aedan weighed the possibilities.

Noah had interacted with him in Halle's dream.

Halle definitely gave him reason to question her origins even before this information presented itself.

And there had been red flags since the moment he had arrived back in the states with orders from Osiris.

So many factors to consider.

"Jess, right now I don't know what Noah was, but I'm betting he wasn't being guarded by one of us."

Jess considered Aedan's conclusion. "You think the Sanhedrin really had a Latibré on him?"

"Why else would Darius be so secretive? Nothing else makes sense. No one knows who is Latibré and who isn't unless you are directly involved with them and even then it's questionable. If Noah was being guarded by one of them and he had the book Apollo and Keros are after, this is going to get nasty. Fast."

Chapter Five

It was Tuesday afternoon before Halle got an email from Toby with the translations from her birthday present. She was curious to know how close her own amateur attempts had come, but the one she was most interested in was the translation of the phrase inscribed on the base of her angel.

She gave a quick scan until she found the one she wanted at the end.

Fallaces sunt rerum species. Somnis vide infra claustrum.

Appearances are deceptive. Look inside for the key to dreams.

"Wow." She smiled at how parallel her research had been to the actual translation.

"What are you wowing about?" Jenna stuck her head in Halle's door before walking in and pouncing onto the bed.

"I just got my translations back from Uncle

T."

"Oh, from the decrepit museum book?"

Halle laughed. "Yep."

"Awesome. What did they say?" Jenna sat up to peer over Halle's shoulder as she read them aloud to her.

"Let's see." Halle glanced over the Latin. "I am so not going to try to read all these phrases and totally butcher them. I'll just tell you what they mean."

"Fair enough." Jenna focused on the screen.

Halle started reading down the list.

"At the threshold of the Apostles, lift your faces to the Light. Hebrews 12:2

Begin here in the presence of the people, within a place for repentance. Matthew 18:20

Faith is to believe what you do not see; the reward of this faith is to see what you believe. Mark 9:23

The one who dreams holds the key. Revelations 1:19

One book leads to another, yet they are the same. Habakkuk 2:2

The appearances of things are deceptive. From the cross, that which is hidden shall be revealed. I John 4:1

I call the living, I mourn the dead. Isaiah 43:1"

Halle mulled the phrases over for a bit. "Well, those are rather cryptic."

Jenna was still studying the phrases on the screen. "They are cryptic, for sure." Her voice didn't hold any of the expected undertones. She was focused and intent. "What's with the Bible verses?"

"No idea. They weren't even written in Latin. Uncle T said they were Hebrew." Halle looked over her shoulder at Jenna. "What's that pensive look about?"

Jenna laughed. "Pensive? Listen to you with the big words."

"It was on my calendar today. So, spill it, what were you thinking about so hard?"

"Nothing. It's just weird that the phrases were Latin and the verses were Hebrew, don't ya think?"

Halle nodded. "Uncle T said the same thing. I wish I could see the book Dad used to have. I wonder if his had mysterious phrases written in it too."

"I'd like to see it myself." Jenna pulled herself away from the computer. "What's that last one, Hal?" She pointed to the phrase at the bottom of the email.

"Oh, that's what is inscribed on the base of the angel Dad got for me."

Jenna looked around, stood, and walked

over to pick it up. "This one?"

"Yeah."

She turned it over and read the Latin phrase aloud. "What does it mean again?"

Halle read it from the email. "Appearances are deceptive. Look inside for the key to dreams."

"Again with the cryptic." Jenna continued rolling the angel gently around in her hands.

"Yeah. It kind of is, huh?"

"I wonder what he meant by it." Jenna mumbled, still studying the angel carefully turning it in circles.

"I don't know. Maybe just some fatherly advice. You know, look inside yourself to find your dreams?"

"Maybe." Jenna sat the angel back on the dresser. "Or maybe there's more to it." She brushed her fingers gently across the angel's wings.

Halle thought about the dream with her dad telling her to read the inscription. Instinct gnawed at her a little, whispered that Jenna was right, there was more to it.

"Anyway." She pushed the gnawing aside. "Friday, after school, Mom's having a little get together before we have our movie marathon with the guys." Halle closed out her email.

"Did you invite Brandt?" Jenna teased.

"No. Even if I did, he has a football game

Friday night. Remember?"

"All the more reason to invite him. You know he'll have to say he can't and you still look interested because you invited him. Do I have to think of everything?"

"That reminds me, what were you two talking about after school today?"

Jenna acted innocent. "You saw that, huh?"

"I did. Care to share?"

"It was nothing really. He just asked me what kind of chance I thought he stood with you."

Halle's curiosity piqued. "Really? And just what did you tell him?"

"I told him to just be himself and be sincere. It would all work out."

"Is that what you think will happen?"

Jenna laughed. "I have no idea. His guess is as good as mine on this one. But you know, you could invite him along Saturday night."

"You are determined. I'll give you that." Halle rolled her eyes at Jenna. "Besides, don't you want me to enjoy my birthday bash since you're the one making me endure it anyway?"

"You only turn eighteen once, Hal. I just want you to have fun."

"You just want a reason to buy a new dress. Admit it." She grinned at her best friend.

"I really am looking forward to shopping in Charlotte Saturday. While we are there, I thought we'd check out that place with all the masks and theatrical costumes too. Maybe we'll find something cool for Levi's Halloween Ball."

"Absolutely, we can do that. I'm definitely going to need a mask."

"Hey, speaking of that, did you ask your mom about the dress in the attic?"

"Yeah. It was my Nana Lisleigh's. Mom said I could wear it. I just need to try it on to make sure it fits."

"We can do that now. So you'll know before we go shopping this weekend. C'mon." Jenna pulled Halle from her chair all the way to the attic.

Aedan wasn't about to hang around while Halle and Jenna played dress up. He was much more concerned with finding out what Darius had learned while he was gone and touching base with Jess regarding his Hellion stake out on the opposite side of the lake.

Aedan pressed the doorbell and waited for Sapphira to let him in. "Why on earth are you ringing the doorbell?" Her green eyes bore into him when she opened the door.

He laughed. "I just wanted to make you wonder who it was."

A relieved smile threaded across her lips. "Now that's the Aedan I know and love. Aggravating soul that you are."

He smiled.

"Can we keep this one? The brooding, serious Aedan isn't my favorite of your personalities." She quipped.

"Yeah, yeah, yeah. Is Darius back yet?"

"He's in the game room."

"Game room? Since when do you have a game room?"

"Since Jess challenged Philip to darts. From there it became pool and now there's an electronic basketball tournament going on."

"Really? Maybe I should put you on Halle duty so I can play with the guys."

She shook her head. "Boys will be boys. I have things to do. He's in there." She pointed to an open door.

Darius was throwing darts at the board across the room. "Hey, Aedan. Care to try?" He held out two darts.

Aedan took the darts and rolled one around between his fingertips while Darius aimed his last shot.

"I guess I know why you're here." Darius said as he released the shot and watched it hit precisely in the center.

"What can you tell me?" Aedan took a

stance in front of the target.

"Noah's Guardian has no idea where the book is."

Aedan released a shot and turned his attention fully to the conversation. "Darius, I think there are a few things you need to know. In return, there are a few things I'd like to know."

"I'm listening."

"I've seen Halle's dreams." Aedan wasted no time.

"You've what? You know how many problems dream walking can cause." A long, slow breath escaped his lips. "So, what have you seen?"

"Well, for starters, they aren't at all what you would expect."

That statement warranted Darius' complete attention. "What do you mean?"

"She can see me, Darius. Noah, too. He was there and he spoke to me. Now, I know there's more going on here than you're telling me. You want to fill me in, or am I going to have to find out my way?"

Darius motioned for Aedan to take a seat in one of the dark leather club chairs in a corner of the room. He sat opposite him.

"As I'm sure you have already gathered, Noah was being protected by the Latibré. The book, according to Noah's Guardian, contains information that would lead to undeniable evidence that could destroy everything Lucifer has worked to build in this realm. Luce will stop at nothing to keep that from happening. He knows there is no redemption for him and he intends to take all of humanity down with him."

Aedan laced his hands together and leaned forward resting his arms on his knees. "How does Halle fit into all of this?"

"That's what we've been trying to figure out. First we thought maybe Noah had left the book for her and Lana might have it packed away with Noah's belongings, but in the last few days, we've learned that isn't the case. Noah must have known the Hellions were aware of its existence and hid it."

"Wait a minute." Aedan interrupted him. "You're telling me Noah knew about the Hellions?"

Darius nodded.

"Does that mean he knew about us as well?"

Another nod from Darius confirmed it. "How?"

"That part we aren't sure of. You know throughout time there have been a few who have been gifted with the knowledge of what occurs in our realm as well as those who have been given the gift of foresight. Some have even been chosen to communicate with us to share our messages."

"Very few, from what I understand." Aedan was still processing the information.

"Of course, there are other theories."

Aedan ran through any logical alternatives. None came to mind. "Like?"

"Like maybe he was one of us."

"That isn't possible." Aedan was certain it wasn't possible.

"Maybe it isn't probable, but all things are possible Aedan, God doesn't work in impossibilities. Regardless, the book is out there and we have to find it, before Apollo does. Because if Apollo finds it, Luce finds it."

"How do you suggest we do that?"

"A source tells me that the book Halle received might have some helpful information in it. We just have to get that information and decipher it."

"Decipher it? Is it in code or something?" Any Guardian could read any language, just as they could speak and understand any language. There shouldn't be anything to decipher.

"It seems the information isn't all in one place and is somewhat, enigmatic."

"You want me to find out what's in Halle's book." It was a statement. There wasn't any need to ask.

"Yes. But I don't think that's going to be

enough. The book Noah had, according to his Guardian, has a lock that I won't be able to open with my ability to manipulate mechanisms. We need to find that key too."

After a few moments of processing the information, Aedan stood from the chair. "I just have two questions."

"Ask."

"Who on this assignment knows about this?"

"Right now, just us. Jess will be filled in when he returns." Darius eyed Aedan curiously. "What's your second question?"

His mouth curved, his voice spilled out mischievously. "Does that blanket permission for no holds barred still exist?"

Darius knew he would likely regret it, but he answered with the orders Osiris had given him. "Do what you need to do, Aedan."

Chapter Six

That night Halle fell asleep clutching the mysterious book to her chest. Aedan contemplated attempting to remove it from her grasp, but decided against it. The last thing he needed was for her to wake up and find him hovering over her, looking like he was after more than the book. He couldn't think of a single scenario where that would end well. His only option was to sit and wait. Not his strong suit.

The green glow of the clock by the bed read 1:33 when Aedan's patience ran out. Halle still had a tight grip on the book, but he couldn't handle just sitting there another moment. He felt like he had to do something. He had been avoiding Halle's dreams for a reason. Now reasons to enter outweighed personal ones to stay out. If Noah was there, maybe he was more than just a dream; maybe he was a source of information. They needed all the information they could get.

Aedan closed his eyes and stepped into the realm where he could interact with Halle without stirring up questions neither of them could answer. Once inside, he found himself standing in a beam of light that shone through a large set of half open wooden doors. He recognized the carvings right away. How could she be here? How could she even know about a place that had never felt the footsteps of humanity?

He stepped through the open doorway to find Halle standing with her back to him, talking to her father. Just the person he was hoping to see. Aedan was about to take a step forward when Noah turned to walk away, but not before he acknowledged Aedan with a nod. Before Aedan could say a word, he was gone.

"Well this was helpful." He muttered to himself.

Halle turned at the sound of his voice. "He knows you. How?" Her gaze turned steely and accusatory. "And why do you keep showing up in my dreams?"

She caught Aedan off guard. Why was she attacking him? She was the one in a sacred chamber no human had set foot in, that he was aware of. His instinct shot back.

"This is your dream. How am I supposed to know the answers to those questions?" He took a confident step toward her causing her to take a step back. He looked around. "What is this place?" Maybe there were some answers to be found, even if they didn't pertain directly to the book.

She looked at him confused. "How am I supposed to know?"

He paused, staring at her with an expression she couldn't quite read. "It's your dream. You're supposed to know." His indignant tone cut through her.

"It's a *dream*. I don't know you and you keep showing up. I have them all the time about places I don't know. I was in ancient Egypt just last week. Watching you, of all people."

Aedan tilted his head. "Me? In Egypt?"

"Yeah." Her tone grew soft. "You and a small dark haired boy." Sadness filled her eyes as she remembered the pain in his face, the lifeless boy in his arms. She watched a flash of that same pain ripple across his features. The irritation he'd provoked disappeared. Something stirred inside, instead of the urge to throw a drink in his face and walk away like before, she found herself wanting to reach out and comfort him.

He pushed the memory away and deliberately shifted his thoughts back to the present. "What else do you dream about that you supposedly have no knowledge of?" His sharp tone returned as he unconsciously gravitated toward her.

He was standing entirely too close. Halle could feel the electricity dance across her skin. Every instinct in her wanted to take a step back; she took one forward instead.

"You. Obviously." Her heart skidded and scrambled inside her chest.

He lingered a few moments, evaluating her reaction, savoring her indignation. The quickening of her pulse brought a smile to his face, one that held a hint of masculine satisfaction. He took another step closer. "Well, Halle, you could always stop dreaming about me, you know."

Her name sounded different on his tongue. She bit down on her lower lip, held her breath, and waited. When he took another step, closing what was left of the gap between them, she narrowed her eyes and peered up at him. He was close enough that she felt the warmth of his shallow breathing on her skin.

"I can't." She whispered.

Aedan felt a binding sense of truth in her words. He searched her eyes. What he saw, he knew would haunt his soul forever. He pulled back, his breath seesawing in his chest.

The hint of confusion in his blue gaze compelled her to explain. "I don't have any control over my dreams." She said softly. "They just take over." Her stare fell to the floor. "They even seem to be taking over my reality too."

Aedan had suspected that after the incident in the park. He had no way of knowing how often it happened, but he had seen enough of Halle's dreams to know she might not survive the ending that never arrived in some of them. She lifted her gaze to meet his, blinking back tears. At that moment, it no longer mattered whose side she was on. The idea of a world without her wasn't a possibility he was willing to allow.

Chapter Seven

"Mr. Yelverton." The static filled voice boomed through the intercom, stopping Coach Yelverton mid-sentence. "Could you please send Halle Michaels to the office?"

"Will do." He responded.

Jenna shot Halle a mocking raised eyebrow. Halle shrugged her shoulders in response.

"Halle, don't forget we start the reports on Monday. Have a topic idea ready." Coach Yelverton returned to reminding the class of their partner assignments while Halle gathered her books to leave. She glanced at the clock on the wall, wondering if she'd even make it to the office before the final bell of the day rang and the halls swarmed with people, and voices.

As far as birthday's ranked, the day had been a pretty good. It started with a serenade from Lana precisely at 6:47 a.m., just like every year, and a candle topped chocolate-chocolate chip muffin, followed by her favorite omelet, the traditional walk down the boulevard of birthday's past, and a present to open.

As far as spending a birthday at school goes, no complaints. There was a substitute in Calculus, which was the best birthday present Mrs. Hester could have given and second period English was a discussion on Shakespeare's *Romeo and Juliet*. Not her favorite Shakespearean play. She never did understand how everyone dying at the end made it such a great love story. She related to Hamlet more anyway. He heard voices.

Lunch was lunch. The only topic around the table was the big get together for Saturday at The Glass House, courtesy of Jenna the party planner, and the even bigger Masquerade Ball at Levi's the following weekend for Halloween. Naturally there were a few comments about Halle's date with Brandt, but Jenna changed the subject before Matt got to the table.

Since Mrs. Barrow had caught wind of it being Halle's birthday, there had been the traditional free day in Art class so she sat in her favorite spot by the window, sketching and watching the rain until Zoe Fisher made a comment about the gorgeous guy she was drawing. "Looks like Brandt has some competition." She had said.

No doubt that would end up in the grapevine before it was all said and done.

Now, here it was the end of the school day and she was no doubt going to pick up birthday flowers from Lana in the office. When she spotted the enormous arrangement through the office window, she couldn't help but think Lana had outdone herself. They were her favorites, calla lilies, mixed with an array of bright pink and yellow flowers.

Mrs. Jenkins eyed her curiously when she walked through the door. "Hi Halle. Special occasion?"

Halle smiled at the vibrant, round faced woman with silver hair and animated brown eyes. "Yes ma'am. It's my birthday."

"Oh, well, Happy birthday dear."

"Thanks." Halle reached for the card. "They're probably from my mom."

Mrs. Jenkins smiled sweetly and continued typing.

When Halle pulled the card from the envelope, her eyes widened. Lana hadn't sent them.

As far as Jenna was concerned, it was bad enough that she had to carry Halle's book-bag to Matt's car because of the flowers, but Halle not revealing what was written on the card was just adding salt to the wound.

"If it starts raining again before Matt gets here to unlock the doors, I'm leaving you on your own." Jenna argued until they reached the Jeep. She placed her book-bag on the bumper and leaned against it staring intently at Halle, waiting for a response.

"What?" Halle knew what she wanted.

"You know. Where is it?"

"Where's what?" Halle feigned ignorance.

"I will absolutely go through everything in this book-bag and your purse right here in this parking lot. Stop torturing me." Jenna was serious.

Halle laughed. "Fine, it's in the side pocket of my purse." She turned so Jenna could reach it.

After reading it Jenna's eyebrows shot up. "Well alright then."

"I know, right?" Halle smiled. "And I haven't seen him at all today. Not even at lunch."

"Looks like that's about to change." Jenna said, her eyes darting in the direction of Brandt's approach.

Halle turned as he walked up, hands in his pockets and a nervous smile on his face. "Happy Birthday, Halle."

"Thanks." She replied shyly. "And thank you for these flowers. They are stunning."

"They pale in comparison, I assure you."

Jenna was behind Brandt at this point, trying to allow some semblance of privacy, but still close enough to give Halle a thumbs up with her right hand and mouth "smooth" before winking and backing away.

Halle blushed a little but hid it by pulling the flowers to her face and taking in the scent. "How did you know callas are my favorite?"

He gave a flirtatious wink. "I have my ways." Brandt was about to ask Halle about date number two when he noticed Matt walking across the parking lot.

"I need to go, but I hope you have a great birthday." He leaned in and kissed Halle on the cheek. "I'm looking forward to seeing you tomorrow night."

She nodded and watched as he walked back to the school.

Matt raised an eyebrow as he unlocked the doors to the Jeep. "I take it those are from the degenerate fleeing the scene of the crime?"

"Yes they are!" Jenna offered enthusiastically. "Are they not absolutely gorgeous? Bet they cost a pretty penny too."

"It's the thought that counts." Halle said quietly, knowing Jenna was right. Callas were out of season.

The ride home from school was typical. Jenna jabbed back and forth with Matt, rambled on about what time Matt and Levi would be at Halle's to watch movies, and reminded them both what time they were leaving on Saturday for The Glass House. Halle listened and responded when necessary. Her mind wasn't on her birthday, or movie night or The Glass House. She kept thinking about him. No matter how she had tried not to, he had been there in every thought since the dream Sunday night. It didn't help that he was real. Knocking her to the ground physically had more than proven he was not just some dream. Even awake, she could close her eyes and feel the electricity skitter across her skin just thinking about him being so close.

"Hal? You listening?" Jenna was staring at her.

"Sorry. What?"

"Levi can't stay for movies tonight. Something he has to help his brother with." Matt glanced at her from the rearview mirror.

"Oh, well that sucks." Halle was getting used to Levi being part of the group.

"Tell me about it." Matt smiled. "Means I'm once again outnumbered in the hormone category."

Jenna smacked his arm. "You know you love us."

"Hey, driving here."

"Stop your whining or we'll make you watch *Hope Floats* again." Halle threatened.

He recovered quickly with his girliest voice. "You guys are the bestest friends ever."

Jenna pinched his cheek playfully. "That's more like it."

Matt pulled into Halle's driveway and put the Jeep in park. "Do ya'll need any help with anything?"

"Nope. I have the flowers. Jenna has the book-bags. I think we're good. Thanks though. See ya at five."

"Don't forget to bring 2 movies." Jenna reminded him. "Otherwise you're stuck watching what we pick out." She grinned at him.

Matt gave a nod in acknowledgment and backed out of the driveway.

Halle noticed the new neighbors sitting on their porch. She shifted the flowers around to one arm and waved.

Jenna held the door open. Halle was hit with the aroma of cake the moment she stepped in the house.

"Mmmm. That smells awesome!" Halle sat her flowers on the table.

Lana came in from the living room to greet the girls. "Ohhh, wow. Who are those from?"

"Brandt." Jenna chimed.

"They are beautiful." Lana leaned in to smell one of the yellow roses. "Seems Mr. Lucas really knows how to play the game, doesn't he?"

Jenna's voice echoed from inside the fridge. "I'd have to say that's an understatement." She emerged with a bottle of water and held it up, a nonverbal to see if Halle wanted one. She shook her head for no. "You should read the card Ms. M! Very creative."

"This I'd like to see." Lana held her hand out.

Hall sighed, pulled the card from her purse and placed in Lana's hand as she walked past. "I'm going to put my things in my room."

Jenna stayed to see Lana's reaction when she pulled Brandt's CPR Certification card from the envelope along with the note card that read "Hopefully being certified will help my chances. Happy Birthday."

Lana cracked up. "Oh, that's priceless."

71

"Isn't it?" Jenna grinned. "He's good. I'll give him that."

"Maybe she'll actually let him kiss her next time." Lana laughed.

"I bet he's a good kisser. He looks like he'd be a good kisser."

Halle called down from the top of the stairs. "I can hear you!"

"Good!" Jenna called back.

Halle bounced back down the stairs. "You both really need to grow up."

Lana smiled and handed Halle the cards and envelope. "I need you two to run over to your house Jenna and get that cake plate your mom said I could borrow if you don't mind."

"What happened to our cake plate?" Halle asked.

"Mrs. Atkins from church still has it from when she was sick a few weeks ago." Lana pulled some napkins and silverware from a drawer. "Oh, and I invited the new neighbors, Hal."

Jenna lit up. "Sweet. I get to meet the neighbors."

"Not just the neighbors. Sapphira's brother is coming with them, too. When she said he'd be over I told her to just bring him along."

Halle inhaled deeply. "Who all is coming, Mom?"

"Matt, Maggie and Lance, of course Pam

and Steve. You said Levi would be here, right?" Lana waited for an answer.

"Yeah. He can't stay for movies, but he'll be here for cake." Halle helped Lana fold the napkins while they talked.

Lana paused before turning to Jenna. "You're being quiet."

Jenna smiled. "Oh, I was just wondering if Sapphira's brother is as hot as her husband."

Lana shook her head. "Of course you were. Okay, I've got this, you guys go get the cake plate. I need that pretty soon."

After the cake plate run, they proceeded to the Haven to set up for the movie marathon.

"What were you thinking?" Aedan couldn't believe what Sapphira expected him to do.

"I was thinking it might be easier to find out what we need to know if you could actually talk to her. You know . . . talking. It's that thing two people do to get to know each other."

"Why couldn't you talk to her?"

"Seriously? Why would she want to talk to her married neighbor?" She glared at him. "You, on the other hand, are my very handsome little college boy brother who will be able to hold her attention much better than me."

Aedan ripped his hand through his hair, frustrated. "I haven't had to hold form for such an extended period of time yet. What happens if I just disappear?"

A smile perked across her face. "I think you'll be just fine."

"Really? I don't know how you can be so sure."

"I know your motivation." She suppressed a smirk.

"What?" Genuine confusion grew in his stare.

"Your motivation. What you think of that pushes you to change form. What you want most." She looked at him, waiting for a response. None came. "Aedan, Darius taught me the same way. Focus on what you want and push as if you are going after it. After a while, it becomes second nature. But even in the beginning stages of controlling it, when what you want is right in front of you . . . it's effortless."

His brows furrowed. How could she possibly know what he wanted?

"It's almost time for the party, brother dear. You might want to change clothes. First impressions and all." She turned to leave and paused at the door. "Oh, and Aedan."

"What?"

"You're welcome." She winked and left Aedan in the room to contemplate what he was about to get himself into.

Voices from the kitchen alerted Halle and Jenna that they had been trying to decide on movies longer than they realized. Jenna pulled out her phone and checked the time.

"Crap. It's 4:20."

Halle placed the movies by the TV and headed for the door. "I have got to change clothes and touch up my makeup. You know Mom is going to be taking pictures. I'll have to look at them for the rest of my life."

"Good point." Jenna followed her down the hall.

Five minutes later Lana was calling the girls down.

"Be right there, Mom." Halle answered. She stood in front of the mirror. "Okay, how do I look?"

Jenna scoffed. "Old."

"Funny." Halle tossed a brush at her. Jenna caught it.

"Seriously, you look great. Stylish, but not overdone. Perfect for birthday photos that you want to look good in, but don't want to look like you tried too hard."

"Awesome. Just the look I was going for. You look smashing as well. Now, c'mon. I think I hear your parents downstairs."

Jenna was showing Halle a text message from Jessica as they walked into the dining room where Lana had set up the decorations and refreshments.

Lana cleared her throat to get the girls' attention. "Halle, you remember Philip and Sapphira." Halle and Jenna both looked up from the phone. Lana looked to the guests. "This is Jenna, Halle's best friend." They exchanged handshakes and hellos.

Halle glanced around expecting the third guest. About that time he walked in from the kitchen and Lana introduced him.

"This is Sapphira's brother, Aedan." Jenna dropped her phone. Halle stood there motionless.

After a moment, Lana took a step toward Halle and placed a hand on her arm to silently urge her to greet the new guest. Halle glanced at her mom and put her hand out.

"Ummm. We've met."

Aedan returned the gesture to be polite. When their hands touched Halle locked stares with him. The electric surge was just like the one in her dream. She jerked her hand back out of surprise.

"Nice to see you again, Halle. Under better

circumstances." He took a few steps backwards and stood by Sapphira who was giving him a strange look.

"How do you two know each other?" Sapphira asked, eyeing them both back and forth.

Aedan never took his eyes from Halle. "Last weekend, in the park –"

Halle interrupted. "He tackled me." Her eyes sparked with amusement.

Aedan smiled back. "Yeah, sorry about that. Again."

"Oh." Sapphira seemed surprised. "I hadn't heard about that."

Lana glanced back at Aedan. "Well, what a small world. I suppose I should thank you, Aedan. Halle doesn't always think before she reacts. She could have been hurt or worse." Lana smiled sincerely. "Thank you."

Aedan focused on Halle before turning back to Lana. "It was my pleasure, Mrs. Michaels."

Jenna stepped forward. "Hi, we didn't get to officially meet last Friday. I'm Jenna." She placed her hand out until Aedan complied.

"Hi Jenna." Aedan smiled politely.

Lana nudged Halle with her elbow, breaking her gaze with Aedan. She couldn't believe he was in her house.

Lana gave her the motherly expression that

reminded her to be hospitable. Halle suggested everyone take a seat around the large table that was typically only used on holidays and occasions when Lana entertained for work.

Philip broke the awkward silence. "The flowers in the kitchen are beautiful."

Jenna glanced at Aedan before she spoke as she sat down. "They're from Brandt. A guy Halle's dating."

"One date." Halle interjected.

"My, those are some pretty amazing flowers for only one date. He must really like you." Sapphira smiled at Halle.

"Or he's overcompensating." Aedan mumbled as he pulled out the chair across the table from Halle.

Sapphira scolded him with a look. "Aedan, why don't you give Halle the gift we brought for her."

The small box in his hand was almost unnoticeable. It wasn't that the box was tiny, but the size of his hand covered it. He slid his hand across the table, pushing the box toward her.

"Silly me had left it on the counter. That's why Aedan had left. He went back to get it. I do hope it suits you." She said sweetly.

Something about Philip and Sapphira made Halle very comfortable. Lana was right when she'd said they seem like old friends. "I'm sure it will."

Halle smiled and looked to Lana for permission to open it.

"Go ahead."

A few rips of the paper revealed a glass box with a beautiful silver cuff bracelet inside.

"Wow." Halle said as she opened the box. "It's amazing."

"It's a prayer of protection cuff." Aedan pointed to the engraving. "It's written in Hebrew."

"It's gorgeous. I love it." Halle slid it onto her wrist. It fit as if it was made for her. "Thank you all so much."

Philip gave a little background about the prayer of protection and the history behind it. Halle listened and tried to stay focused on what Philip was saying, but her eyes kept glancing back to the dark indigo eyes staring at her from across the table. She was somewhat relieved when the rest of the guests arrived.

Matt and Levi congregated with Aedan on one side of the table. Lana insisted that Halle move to the head of the table since it was her birthday. Lana led the group in singing and waited for Halle to make a wish. Jenna saw the eye contact between Halle and Aedan just before Halle blew out the candles.

After cake and presents Lana and Maggie began the clean-up. Everyone pitched in and in no time the dining room was left empty with the exception of balloons and streamers. In Lana fashion, those wouldn't come down until after 6:47 a.m. the following day.

Levi was second to leave, right after Jenna's parents. He thanked Halle and Lana for inviting him and apologized for not being able to stay. "Happy birthday, Hal."

"Thanks Levi. Sorry you can't stay and hang out." Halle walked him to the door.

"Me too. I'll see ya tomorrow night though." He waved and headed to his car.

Lana and Maggie were talking to Sapphira in the kitchen while Matt, Philip and Aedan were still sitting around the dining room table.

Halle glanced from room to room. "Where's Jenna?"

Matt answered from the dining room. "She went upstairs to get the TV set up."

"Oh. Okay."

"Hey Aedan, you should stay and watch movies with us." Matt suggested and then glanced to Halle as if he'd forgotten to ask permission and wanted to make sure he hadn't totally screwed up.

"I don't want to intrude." Aedan tried not to look at Halle.

Matt, on the other hand, glared straight at her.

"You are more than welcome to stay,

Aedan." Halle assured him. Every cell in her wanted him to stay.

"C'mon man, it would even the odds for me." Matt pleaded. "The more testosterone, the less likely I have to watch Audrey whats-her-name movies."

Aedan laughed. "What? I loved *Breakfast at Tiffany's.*"

Matt threw his head back dramatically. "Halle, you should marry this guy." He laughed and shook his head. "Aedan, you may not be much help to me after all."

"I'm barely legal and you're already trying to marry me off? Don't let Mom hear you say that." Halle smiled and turned to Aedan. "Seriously, though. We'd love for you to stay if you'd like."

"Of course he would." Sapphira placed a hand on Halle's shoulder. "Don't let him tell you otherwise. He's just trying to be polite." She turned her attention to Aedan. "It's either stay here and watch movies with them or come home with us and watch Philip flip between documentaries."

"Movies it is." Aedan laughed.

"Hey." Philip spoke up. "Documentaries are informational."

Everyone just shook their heads.

"Of course they are honey." Sapphira winked at him.

"Well, I think we are going to head home. Halle, thank you for letting us share your birthday with you." Sapphira leaned in and hugged Halle tightly.

"Thank you again for the bracelet. I love it." Halle smiled.

"Thank Aedan. It was his idea." Sapphira beckoned Philip with a look.

Halle thanked Philip and walked them both to the door. When she turned around she almost lost her balance trying to avoid colliding with Aedan's chest. He reached for her arm to steady her.

"Sorry." He said, fighting to ignore the ache touching her brought on.

"It's ok."

"I seem to have a presupposition for knocking you down." His crooked smile sent her pulse into overdrive.

"A presuppa-what?" She chuckled at him. "That must be one of those words they teach you to use in college, huh?"

"Something like that."

Halle realized he was taller than she had originally thought. He was quite the presence standing there in the small mudroom.

"I just wanted to say thanks." His dark eyes held a glint of something alluring.

"For?" Her vocabulary had been reduced to

one syllable responses.

"Making me feel welcome. Inviting me to hang out with you." He was doing that thing again, where he was close enough she could hear him breathe.

She smiled. "Anytime." Three syllables. It was an improvement.

"Hey Hal, movies rea – oh. Sorry." Jenna turned on her heel and started back through the kitchen.

"Coming." Halle called to Jenna, eyes still fixated on Aedan. "You ready?"

"After you." He stepped to the side and gestured his arm for her to pass.

One phone call from Uncle Toby and two and a half movies later, Jenna and Halle both were asleep. Matt and Aedan were finishing the end of *The A Team* and talking about special effects when Matt threw Aedan for a loop.

"You know, you should ask Halle out."

"Uhh, didn't Jenna say she was dating someone? The flowers guy?"

Matt laughed. "She went on one date with him. Besides, he's a complete tool."

The questioning look told Matt he might

have to explain. "He's not what I would consider a good guy for Halle, or really any girl for that matter. He's been around the block a few too many times and his moral standards aren't really up to speed with hers."

"Ahhh. So why is she going out with him then?" Aedan was genuinely curious.

"The guy is smooth. I mean, did you see those flowers?" Matt seemed irritated. "He knows what to say and how to say it."

"What if she really likes him?"

Matt grinned and shook his head at Aedan's cluelessness. "Man, did you not see the way she was looking at you tonight?"

Jenna groaned a little and shifted until her head was resting on Matt's arm. He looked down at her, suppressing a smile.

Aedan watched Matt for a moment. "Mind if I ask you a question?"

"Sure."

"Why haven't you asked Jenna out?"

Matt didn't hesitate. "Because it's Jenna."

Aedan grinned. "Do you not see the way she looks at you?"

Matt tilted his head in disbelief. Looked down at the platinum blonde asleep on his arm then back up to respond to Aedan. "Man, its Jenna. She's been one of my best friends for years. Even if I had thought about it, what if I did and it didn't work out. Then I've ruined one of the best friendships I've ever had."

Aedan considered the logic in Matt's reasoning, he'd never had the chance to discuss why mortals made the choices they made until now. A smile snaked up one corner of his mouth, as he looked over at Halle asleep on a throw pillow beside him.

"I see the way you look at her, too, ya know." A knowing look spread over Matt's face.

"What makes you think I'm any more morally up to par than the other guy?" A spiral of hair lay across Halle's face. Aedan fought the urge to reach over and brush it aside. He turned his attention back to Matt.

"Gut feeling." Matt responded.

"She doesn't even know me."

"I think we can fix that. That is, if you want to." Matt's expression was a question, waiting for an answer. When Aedan didn't respond quickly enough, Matt nodded his head. "I'm going to take that as a yes. Tomorrow night. If you have plans, change them. You're coming out with us."

Chapter Eight

Halle woke up in her bed at 2:51 a.m. in a panic, still wearing the yoga pants she had put on halfway through the second movie. She couldn't remember watching the end of the last movie, the guys leaving, or how she got to her room. She was certain she had dreamt Aedan carried her there, but that was pushed aside by the dream that had awakened her.

It was so real. She was still gasping for air. The dream had her running as though her life depended on it. Deep down, she knew it had.

Reaching for the lamp, she tried to calm her breathing, calm herself. After jotting down the dream, she thought about the whirlwind her life had turned into over the last eight weeks. She lay there, silently praying. *God, I don't know what's going on. I don't know if I'm losing it or if you're trying to tell me something. If it's you, I'd appreciate a little more of a direct approach. I'm beginning to think something's seriously wrong with me here. Please. Just do something. Anything. I need some clarity. God, I need to feel like I'm not losing my mind.*

She glanced at the clock.

3 a.m.

With a click, the lamp was off and she settled into her pillows, praying for sweeter dreams.

She rubbed her eyes, and squinted until the clock came into focus. When she noticed the time, she jumped out of bed and quickly made her way to the guest room to wake Jenna.

"Jen. Jen. Wake up." She bounced up and down on the bed beside her.

"What? Go away."

"But Jen. Shopping. Shoes. Masquerade Ball." She drug the last word out.

Jenna sat up in bed, eyes still half closed. "Did you say shopping?"

"Yep. And you know how you wanted to

leave here by 9:30?"

"Yesss."

"Not gonna happen if you don't get up like right now."

"Alright, alright. I'm up. But you're taking me to Starbucks on the way out."

Halle smiled. "Deal. I want a pumpkin spice latte anyway." Halle bounced on the bed again and sprang off to her room.

"That's not even coffee." Jenna called after her.

Thirty minutes later they were sitting in line at the Starbucks drive thru.

"That will be $10.68," the less than perky voice grumbled through the speaker.

"Jen, I have a gift card in my purse. Can you grab it? Should be in the inside pocket."

Jenna rummaged through Halle's purse and pulled out a folded piece of paper. "What's this?"

Halle looked at it, "Oh, that's the email Uncle T sent me with the translations."

Jenna pulled out the card. "Here it is. Coffee's on you!"

Halle smiled, "Technically, it's on you. Your mom and dad gave it to me for my birthday."

"Either way, it's saving me four bucks." Jenna unfolded the paper and read over the translations while they waited in line. "Hey, Hal."

"Yeah?"

"Are these in the order they are written in your book?"

Halle glanced at the paper. "Yeah. The top one was the first one in the book and so on."

"Hmmm." Jenna studied them, read them silently. "Have you wondered who would have written them in a blank journal?"

Halle hadn't thought of the book as a journal, but now that she had, it was easy to see that's exactly what it was. Her dad had written in his. "Yeah, kinda. I keep trying to put two and two together because of Dad's missing journal. I know it sounds all cloak and dagger, but I have this unnerving feeling the two books are connected somehow."

Jenna looked over the paper again. "Well, maybe these phrases have something to do with the connection." She cocked an eyebrow.

Halle pulled up to the window, handed her the card as she took the coffees from the girl at the register, and handed one to Jenna.

Jenna began reading them aloud all together. "That doesn't make sense."

Halle smiled at the girl, said thank you and

drove away from the window. "Maybe they aren't in the right order to make sense. Or maybe they aren't supposed to go together at all. Maybe they are just verses."

Jenna thought about it while Halle drove. "Maybe if we read them alphabetically."

"Alphabetically?"

"Yeah. You know, first letter of each phrase."

"Hey. Give it a shot."

Jenna pulled a pencil from Halle's purse and wrote numbers beside them to put them in order. "At the threshold of the Apostles, lift your faces to the Light. Hebrews 12:2

Begin here in the presence of the people, within a place for repentance. Matthew 18:20

Faith is to believe what you do not see; the reward of this faith is to see what you believe. Mark 9:23

I call the living, I mourn the dead. Isaiah 43:1

One book leads to another, yet they are the same. Habakkuk 2:2

The appearances of things are deceptive. From the cross, that which is hidden shall be revealed. I John 4:1

The one who dreams holds the key. Revelations 1:19"

"That still doesn't give me anything I can

understand." Halle pulled onto the interstate. "Let's try to think about what each one means and then see if rearranging them would help."

Jenna nodded.

"The first one, about the threshold and the Apostles." Halle merged into traffic. "Let's start with that one. We obviously know who the Apostles are. Threshold. That's like a doorway, right?"

Jenna was jotting notes down on the paper. "Yeah. So, at the doorway of the Apostles. The rest seems pretty cut and dry. Lift your face to the light."

"Agreed. What's next?"

Jenna read the next phrase. "Presence of people and place of repentance."

Halle laughed.

"What's funny about that?" Jenna peered over at Halle.

"Well, if we were Catholic the place of repentance would be church. Ya know, confessional."

Jenna noted it on the paper. "Who says the person who wrote these wasn't Catholic?"

"Okay. I see your point. That means the presence of people?"

"Still falls under the church idea."

"So you begin at church." Halle glanced in

the side mirror at the dark grey car that had been behind them since pulling out of Starbucks in Lake Arella. She told herself it was a coincidence and interrupted Jenna's singing. "What are you singing?"

"George Michaels. *Faith*."

Halle laughed. "Ummm... Why?"

"I dunno. The next phrase is about faith, that's what popped in my head. Want me to sing it again? Because I can."

"Nah. I'm good. Just read me the phrase." She smiled.

"Fine, your loss." Jenna was still bopping her head to the mental tune. "Faith is to believe what you do not see; the reward of this faith is to see what you believe." Jenna thought about it. "I don't really think that needs much discussion. Kind of means what it means, doesn't it?"

"Yeah. I guess so. Unless it's meant for something specific. But how are we supposed to know what that would be? Anyway. What's next?"

"I call the living, I mourn the dead." Jenna faked a shiver. "That's just a little creepy sounding."

Halle repeated the phrase a few times quietly, mulling it over. "Why does that seem familiar?"

"Ya know, Hal, the next one sure confirms that gut feeling of yours."

"Meaning?"

Jenna gave an odd look. "One book leads to another, yet they are the same? I'd say that sounds a little like what you said, wouldn't you?"

She turned into the shopping center parking garage and followed the arrows to the numbered parking levels. Something in Halle's mind clicked.

"Jen, maybe we're looking at this all wrong."

"What do you mean? How should we be looking at it?"

"It's about the order, right? Maybe it isn't about the alphabet because it was in Latin. Our alphabet wouldn't matter. It's about the levels, the numbers."

Jenna narrowed her eyes and furrowed her brow. "You aren't making any sense at all. Give it to me in English."

"The verses. They wouldn't change. They weren't even in Latin, but Hebrew. No matter what language they're in, they are in the same order in the Bible. Put the Bible verses in order."

"Man. That's pretty ingenious thinking there. Look at you being all brilliant and such. So, which one comes first?"

She laughed as she parked the car. "I don't know. I'm fairly lost after Deuteronomy and then the New Testament has Matthew, Mark, Luke, and

John. I know Revelations is last. And...yeah. That's all I got."

Jenna rolled her eyes. "What kind of church girl are you?"

"Do you know them in order?" She said with a smile of silent mockery.

"We'll look them up later." Jenna avoided answering.

"Yeah. That's what I thought." Halle grinned.

"Time for shopping."

Aedan wasn't too thrilled with sending Jess to keep an eye on Halle for the day, but Darius had insisted. After Sapphira's scheme to shove Aedan grudgingly into Halle's reality, Darius felt some additional training might not be a bad idea.

"Don't forget, Aedan, in mortal form you can still use your abilities, but you are also more vulnerable to attack. Any damage inflicted will take more than twice the time to heal." Darius followed the reminder with yet another blue flame, hurled effortlessly in Aedan's direction.

Aedan dodged to the side, avoiding the flame by a hair. "Is that the best you've got?"

Darius laughed, "No. But it's getting late

and you have an assignment to get to. If I hurt you now, who would I send?"

"Excuses, excuses." Aedan ribbed before slinging a bolt that grazed the edge of Darius' coat when he didn't move quickly enough.

"I liked this coat."

"Should have been quicker, old man." Aedan smiled.

He walked over to where Aedan stood and placed a hand on his shoulder. "It's good to see you coming back around, Aedan. Now we had best get back before Sapphira comes looking for us. No powers exist to save you from a woman's wrath. A lesson worth remembering."

Halle was dressed and ready to go thirty minutes before time to leave. She had just hung up the phone with Jenna to see how much longer she'd be when she received a text from Lana.

Need a favor on your way out tonight.

Swing by this address and lock the building for me.

I forgot. Door in the back. Thanks Hal. Love you.

1734 Jenson St.

Jenson Street was in the warehouse district

downtown. She hated downtown. Always had a weird vibe when she was there. Lana rarely asked for favors like this, mostly because she rarely forgot things, so when she did Halle responded.

She scrolled through her contacts and touched on Matt's name, grabbed her coat and purse and headed downstairs as the phone dialed.

Matt was giving Aedan all the details for meeting them at The Glass House when his phone rang.

"Hey Hal, what's up? You running late?" He was expecting her to say yes.

"No. I'm actually ready now smarty pants, but I just got a text from mom. I need to run a quick errand for her. I'm going to go ahead and leave and just meet you guys there. Okay?"

"Umm, are you sure, we can see if Jen is ready and go together. I'm over with Aedan right now. He and I are ready."

"She's not ready – wait. You're with Aedan?" Utter shock filled her voice.

"Yes. I invited him to go tonight. He's going to meet us there."

"Oh. Umm. Okay. Well . . . I just talked to Jen like five minutes ago. She was still deciding what to wear."

"You're rubbing off on her punctuality."

"Yeah. That's *all* me. Anyway, I'll see you guys there. Shouldn't take long. I'll be there about the time you are I'd guess."

"Alright then. See you at eight."

"'K. Bye."

"Bye Hal."

Halle was already backing out of her driveway before she'd said goodbye to Matt. Over forty-five minutes later, she was pulling into the vacant lot in front of 1734 Jenson Street. A "for sale" sign in front of the building assured her she was in the right place. The rain storm had slowed her progress and now she was behind schedule. She saw no way to drive around to the rear of the building, which might be why it hadn't sold yet. Who doesn't have a direct access to the back of a building that's almost two football fields long? There was likely access from another street, but she had no idea how to find it in the maze of other alleys and warehouses.

She was going to have to walk to the back. Not something she had planned when she chose to wear heels. If there was a door in the back, she assumed it would be at the end with the offices, so she parked there.

Thankfully the rain had stopped, but the clouds looming overhead blocked any light the almost full moon might have had to offer. She fumbled through the console looking for her flashlight. Of course, the batteries were dead.

As creepy as the parking lot seemed, there was no way she was walking around in the dark. After pulling her coat on and opening the flashlight app on her phone, she stepped into the chilled, damp air. A click of the remote locked the car doors and she shoved the keys into her coat pocket then headed toward the back of the building.

Loading bay doors lined up as far as she could see. Surely Lana didn't mean one of those. Halle walked, shining what little light the phone put off toward the loading docks. She was close to the opposite end of the building when what she thought was an entry door came into view. She climbed the concrete steps leading to it and checked the door. Locked.

"Just call her." Talking to herself aloud made her feel a little less freaked out.

She tapped the flashlight on the phone and pulled up her contacts. It shut down. She tried to reset it. It didn't work. It was dead. She was positive she'd had a full battery when she left the house.

"You have got to be kidding me."

The streetlights three blocks away were barely enough to guide Halle's path. She steadily paced past the shadows of the abandoned loading bays, her feet splashing through the remnants of the storm she could still hear rumbling in the distance. She knew she had made a mistake

98

coming alone. Trying to convince herself that her imagination was getting the better of her, she attempted to ignore the sound of footsteps growing behind her in the alleyway.

Where are the voices now, she thought.

Determined to prove to herself that she was hearing things, she spun around to find she was facing nothing beyond a dull street light fighting its way through the fog that had set in behind the storm. She turned slowly and began walking toward her destination once more, occasionally throwing an uneasy glance behind her, still aware of the footsteps that haunted her, that kept pace with hers. They grew heavier. Once more, she whirled around abruptly but was again met by the emptiness of the shadows.

For the first time in her life, Halle felt alone. Adrenaline fired through her veins. Her heart attacked her chest. She walked faster. The mist grew heavier. She could barely see where her next step would land.

With the footsteps closer now, she was contemplating an all-out run for it when she heard a faint whisper. Not the voice she hoped for. Or longed for. It held nothing comforting or familiar. It was a dark, horrifying voice unlike anything she had ever heard before. Something caused her to stop dead still. She couldn't will herself to move forward even though she tried. The whisper grew louder, repeating a phrase over and over in a language she didn't understand.

An icy charge struck her as she turned slowly to see the hint of a sinister silhouette moving toward her through the fog. The déjà vu slammed into her like a brick wall as the familiar scene played out before her eyes. She stood there paralyzed, waiting for the next moment. The one that had never arrived in her dream. A moment she was suddenly sure could be her last. Closing her eyes, she began to repeat the only words she could manage to form in her terrified mind. *Help me. God. Where are you? I need you. Do something.* Her thoughts raced. Her mind cried out what her voice couldn't. Eyes squeezed tight, she listened, waiting for the footsteps to get closer but they stopped.

She wasn't sure how many times she had repeated the prayer when the agonizing screeches began. Hesitating to open her eyes, expecting it to be her final act, she gave in to morbid curiosity and discovered she was alone. The dark figure that had hunted her through the alley was nowhere to be seen. But what was that tormented noise in the shadows?

A blinding flash of blue light, followed by another bellow of pain echoed from the dark recesses of the alleyway. Everything went white, then pitch black.

Her instinct said run, but she stood there, still unable to move, still unable to see. Where do the blind run to anyway? Before she could take a breath and try to gain some semblance of control, someone, or *something*, had her and they were moving at a speed that churned everything inside her. Her last thought before everything went cold, she prayed death would at least come quickly.

.

Chapter Nine

When she came to, Halle felt like someone had hit her with a two by four. Her head was pounding, she was queasy and the pain in her chest was close to unbearable. To top it off, someone was very lightly stroking her hair, which only caused the pounding to intensify. She tried to open her eyes.

"Halle? Can you hear me?"

That voice, that accent. She knew that accent. Pure confusion took over.

"Aedan?"

She could almost hear the smile in his voice when she said his name.

"Yeah. Are you alright? How are you feeling?"

"I'm not sure. I can't open my eyes, my head is killing me, and..." She tried to move. "Everything hurts. What happened?" Panic laced every word.

"Actually, your eyes are open. Just take a deep breath and talk to me, tell me what you remember."

His arms cradled around her and she felt safe, but logically the moment didn't make sense.

"Why, why can't I see anything? Why does it hurt so bad?" She felt the tug of sleep pulling her back in.

"I don't know. Do you remember anything?" His voice was calming, soothing to her. Inside he was anything but calm. A feeling he wasn't familiar with.

She tried to remember what had happened. "I was behind the building, walking back to my car."

His voice held a thrum of anger when he spoke again. "What were you doing in this area? Alone?"

"I, uh . . ." Her head throbbed and she reached to place a hand on her forehead.

His tone dropped, "We have to get you checked out."

He opened a mental link.

"Sapphira, I found her."

"Thank God. Jess said Apollo has put a price on her head, but he wants her alive. Keep your guard up, Aedan. I have no idea what this is about and I don't know how soon before the word is out."

"Yeah, considering the nasty piece of shadow demon I just made friends with, I think it's safe to say the word is already out."

There was a pause before Sapphira responded.

"He didn't touch her, did he?"

"No, I got to him before he got to her, but she needs a doctor or a healer, I'm thinking a healer might be a better option. Do you know of one close enough to contact?"

"What happened? Why is she hurt if he didn't touch her?"

Aedan considered what he knew. He had never heard of a mortal seeing a flash of lux dei before, a weapon also known as "The light of God" which only a fraction of immortals possessed. Even those who possessed the ability had to learn to develop it and that was easier said than done. Most were initially warriors, but after the Great Fall, many of those warriors were called to protect humanity. He wasn't sure what damage that weapon might cause a human. It wasn't something that had ever been tested to his knowledge. The tracing, however, was another issue altogether.

"I'm not 100% sure why she can't see, but...I

traced with her. You know what kind of effect that has had on mortals in the past, and before you say anything, no. I wasn't thinking. I just wanted her out of there."

"How did you find me?" Halle mumbled, interrupting his focus. She teetered in and out of consciousness.

She fell limp in his arms. His heart plummeted. The feel of her life force fading was a punch to the gut.

"Stay with me Halle. Don't you dare give up on me." His voice thick with desperation.

"Sapphira. I need a healer and I need one now. Find one and meet me at the safe house. The old safe house."

"Aedan, you didn't –"

He cut her off. *"I did. Just get someone who can help. Soon, or we're going to lose her."*

Sapphira heard the urgency and panic in his tone. Aedan never panicked. *"I'm on it."*

Halle had been in and out of consciousness for what seemed like an eternity to Aedan before someone arrived.

"What happened?"

The voice startled him. Instinctually, Aedan

whipped around, a ring of lux dei already beginning to form around his free hand. He immediately withdrew it when he saw Darius.

"You're on edge, Aedan. You know the only place safer than right here is Marom itself. Tell me what's going on. I can't help until you do." Darius moved closer to them. Aedan relaxed his hold on Halle.

"This is my fault. I traced with her. I know I shouldn't have. I didn't think. I messed up. Please tell me someone is coming to help her, Darius. Please. We can't lose her." His words rambled out.

Darius couldn't recall ever seeing terror behind Aedan's eyes. He had always been the one student he had trained with no apprehension, no fear. But there it was.

Darius placed a reassuring hand on Aedan's shoulder. "Someone is on the way. Genevieve is a very capable healer, but you will have to leave while she works."

Aedan nodded in acknowledgment.

"Also, we have to get Halle back to the alley and you will have to take Matt and Jenna to find her. We can't blow your cover. You know that."

"I don't want to leave –" Aedan started to protest.

Darius cut him short.

"It isn't a request, Aedan. It's an order. I need you to head back to The Glass House. I'll send you instructions on what to do. Sapphira is taking a car there for you. I'll let you know when Genevieve has completed the healing process and you can put the plan into motion." Darius reached beneath Halle to remove her from Aedan's reluctant arms.

"She's blind too." Aedan half whispered.

"What? How did that happen?"

"I don't know. I didn't think it was possible for humans to see lux dei, but eyesight isn't something that has ever been affected by tracing to my knowledge, that leaves only one logical option. She saw the light from the attack."

At that moment Halle groaned, rolled her head slowly to one side and whispered something.

"What did she say?" Darius asked, trying to listen more closely.

Aedan suppressed a smile and shook his head like he wasn't sure, but he was. He would recognize his name spilling from Halle's lips for eternity, no matter how quietly.

All the nights he had watched her sleep, she'd looked so peaceful; he looked at her now and wished she were only sleeping, not fighting for her life.

"Go, Aedan. Genevieve is ready to trace in."

Chapter Ten

Aedan arrived at The Glass House to find Sapphira waiting in the parking lot beside a dark, metallic blue BMW.

"What's this? This isn't your car." Aedan's stare grazed the sleek lines.

"It's the X6 M. We figured you were going to need your own car." She tossed him the keys. "Any word about Halle?"

He gave a stiff side-to-side headshake.

"I'm sorry, Aedan. I know this must be hard for you after . . ." She trailed off.

Aedan glared at her. "This will *not* be a repeat of Egypt. Halle will be fine. She has to be."

Sapphira tried to smile, but it was thin and forced and Aedan saw right through it. "Egypt changed you. I haven't seen you care about anyone since then." Her voice softened. "You've existed, Aedan. You've done your duty, but every action, every reaction, has been calculated and detached. Until now. I can see that you actually care about her."

"It's easier not to care." His tone was flat.

"But God didn't create us that way. We are meant to care for those we protect, that's what separates us from the likes of Apollo and Keros. God believes in love, Aedan. Remember, we are created in His image in much the same way humanity is. It's okay to care. It's okay to love."

He didn't want to admit that, for the first time in his existence, what he experienced tonight didn't feel like anything he had felt before. It was suffering and anguish wrapped in a devotion he had never expected he could feel toward a mortal. There had always been the knowledge that mortals are a blink in the universe. They were here and then gone. That was accepted, not questioned. Aedan remembered a time when it was difficult to watch them die, but knowing they would leave this world for Marom was comforting. Tonight, the thought of Halle leaving this world was anything but comforting. Even with the knowledge she would wake in Heaven, Aedan couldn't bear that she would be gone. For the first time in his life, he could relate to what the Messiah had felt. Willing to trade his life for a mortal's.

Aedan's words slipped through his teeth. "If anything happens to her, I will hunt Apollo to the ends of the universe. And he will pay for this."

He meant it. Sapphira had no doubt of that. Not wanting to think of the possibility of losing Halle any more than Aedan did, she changed the subject.

"Well, you better get in there. Darius will be sending you your instructions. I'll see you soon." She traced away.

Aedan shoved the keys in his pocket, pushed the thought away, and headed inside reluctantly.

Darius stood back, observing as the petite form stood solemnly beside the body lying on the marble healing slab. Her hands glided slowly in a circular motion over every vital organ, radiating an emerald green glow that appeared to be absorbed into the body.

She stopped when she completed several rotations over Halle's heart.

"What did you say happened with her sight?" She tilted her head and waited for Darius' response.

"Not sure. Aedan said it's a possibility she saw a discharge of lux dei."

Her large hazel eyes widened with curiosity. "Do *you* think that's possible?" She stared at Halle a moment, still unconscious. "If she can see lux dei, imagine the other possibilities." She extended a hand to skim above Halle's eyes.

"Can you heal her eyes as well?" Darius asked.

"I can only do so much without knowing the precise damage. If it was lux dei, they will have to heal on their own." Her voice fell. "If they heal at all. I've never encountered anyone who witnessed such a battle and lived."

"You know that Aedan has voiced his suspicions that she isn't human. You would have better insight into that than anyone. Do you think he could be right?"

Genevieve ran her hands over Halle's eyes once more and considered the possibility before answering. "Physically, everything about her appears human. Inside and out. But I must admit, there are things about her, things that make me question her humanity as well. What I really find fascinating though is how quickly Aedan has caught on to some of the subtleties that have taken years for the rest of us to pick up on. He's very gifted,

Darius. When all of his powers emerge, he will make one B.A. Latibré."

Darius smiled. He knew she was right, he'd known that since he began training Aedan.

Genevieve paused before turning a pensive eye at Darius. "You know she's changing him, don't you?"

He met her stare, waited for her next words.

"She's the reason his abilities are coming to the surface so quickly, but I'm afraid that isn't the only way she's affecting him. There's something else I can't put my finger on. And I have a bad vibe about it. Something tells me this isn't going to end well, for any of us."

"That has crossed my mind." Darius drew a deep breath. "I think the sooner we find that book and get it somewhere safe, the sooner we can all rest a little easier."

"Has the tracker Osiris assigned had any success tracking where Halle's book came from?"

"I haven't gotten a report yet. She's in Egypt now, but should be checking in soon." Darius turned his ear, listening. "Sapphira is here with the car to take Halle back to the alley. I'll stay with her until Aedan can get back to her."

Genevieve nodded. "I increased her melatonin levels; she should sleep long enough to get her back without her waking. Keep me posted."

Darius turned toward his name echoing down the hallway. When he turned back, Genevieve was gone.

"Darius?" Sapphira walked over to Halle, her voice filled with concern as she placed her hand on Halle's head in a motherly manner.

"She's going to be fine," he assured her.

A breath of relief escaped.

"We need to get her back to the alley, though. I'm not sure how much longer she'll sleep."

Darius collected Halle in his arms and followed Sapphira down the hallway and into the night, where the car awaited.

Aedan fought his way through the crowded dance floor scanning for Matt and Jenna. He spotted Matt in the far back corner waving him over. When he arrived at the table, Matt introduced him to everyone. Jessica and Tina immediately began whispering when Aedan turned his back.

"So where are Halle and Jenna?" Aedan looked around. He knew where Halle was, but Jenna needed to be close by. He didn't want to waste time when he received word to go to Halle.

"As usual, Halle isn't here yet. Jenna is

around here somewhere. Probably jabbering to someone."

Aedan glanced at his watch. It was a meaningless gesture, but he was trying to appear more human. "Shouldn't Halle have been here by now? She said she'd meet you here thirty minutes ago, didn't she? I mean, it is her birthday bash, right?" He attempted to keep his tone casual.

Matt pulled his cell phone from his pocket and checked it. "You're right, ten minutes late is just Halle time. She's actually forty-five minutes late. That's not like her." He pressed a few buttons on his phone and held it to his ear. When he heard Halle's voice on the other end, he hung up. "Her phone's going to voicemail."

"Do you know where she was going before coming here?" Just as he asked, Aedan received word from Darius that he and Sapphira were on their way back to the warehouse with Halle.

"No, she said she was running an errand for her mom. I'll call Lana. Why don't you see if you can find Jenna. Halle might be with her."

Aedan scanned the crowd, searching for a head of bright blonde hair. After a couple of false spottings, he saw her on the outside deck talking to someone. He moved as quickly as he could through the crowd to get to her.

"Jenna." He placed a hand on her arm to get her attention.

"Oh, hi Aedan." She glanced back to the guy she was talking to. "This is Brandt. Brandt, this is Aedan."

Brandt held his hand out in greeting.

Aedan's jaw tightened. "Flower guy, right?" He shook Brandt's hand and a strange sensation jolted through him.

Brandt half-squinted one eye, silently weighing the comment.

Jenna grinned.

"So, you know Halle then?" Brandt asked.

Something possessive stirred and before he could stop himself, the words slipped out. "I tucked her in last night, so I guess you could say that." Aedan wished he could have savored the look on Brandt's face, but getting Jenna to listen was more of a priority.

Jenna shook her head at him and tried not to smile.

"Jenna, we need to go." Aedan's tone was urgent.

"What? We just got here."

"I know, but Halle isn't here yet and she isn't answering her phone. We need to find her."

"Did you call Lana?"

"Matt's calling her now."

Brandt interrupted. "I'm coming with you."

Aedan shot a cold glare at Brandt and

looked immediately back to Jenna. "Let's see what Matt found out." Aedan walked away, Jenna and Brandt following in the path he made through the crowd.

The look on Matt's face told Aedan he was concerned before he ever spoke. "Lana said she never sent Halle a message. I don't like this." Matt noticed Brandt as the words escaped and immediately proceeded to pretend he wasn't there.

Jenna could see it was going to be a long night, for Brandt if no one else. He was outnumbered two to one. Clearly Matt, nor Aedan, cared much for his presence.

"Let's go outside where it's quiet and figure out where to start looking." Jenna knew she needed to diffuse the situation and get the focus on finding Halle before the testosterone took over.

They barreled through the mass of dancers, in a straight shot for the exit, bumping people out of the way as they went. Aedan was last to make it to the parking lot.

"Okay, so where do we start?" Matt looked to Jenna.

"I'm thinking," she said, forcing words out past the wheels turning in her head.

"I have an idea." They all looked to Aedan, waiting for his next words. "Philip has a background in certain . . . technologies. Matt, you said Halle's phone rang several times and went to voicemail, right?"

Matt nodded.

"Good. That means it's turned on." Aedan pulled out the cell phone Sapphira had given him earlier in the day. Thankfully, she had also programmed some names and numbers in it. He pressed the button when he got to Philip's name and waited for him to answer. "Philip. It's Aedan. I need you to trace Halle's cell phone and tell me where she is."

Philip asked a few questions just to help save cover, but gave Aedan an address after a few minutes. Aedan hung up the phone and pulled his keys from his pocket. "I got it. Jensen Street. Anyone know where that is?"

Jenna piped in. "I do. It's downtown."

Aedan was already walking toward the blue BMW. "Let's go."

Chapter Eleven

Fifteen minutes later, they were scouring the numbers on street signs looking for the 1700 block of Jensen Street.

"There!" Matt shouted. "There's Halle's Trailblazer."

"I don't like this." Jenna whispered.

Aedan whipped the car into the parking lot. He was parked by Halle's SUV and out of the car before anyone else could get their door open.

He scanned the parking lot for Halle. When he didn't see her he ran to the back of the building and found her lying in the alleyway. A nearby transformer sparked as it cooled. Aedan knew Darius had hit it with lux dei as a cover story. The energy of it still lingered in the air. He had gathered

Halle in his arms before the others even made it to the alley.

Jenna ran to meet him. "Is she okay? What happened?"

"We need to get her to a hospital." Aedan kept walking toward the car. "There's a transformer back there that blew. It's still sparking. Not sure how close she was to it when it did."

Brandt opened the car door as they reached the parking lot. "I'll take her."

Aedan's glare sliced through him. "Jenna, the keys are still in the ignition. You can drive. I'll sit in back with Halle." He carefully slid into the backseat, Halle in his lap, her head resting on his shoulder.

Brandt looked around. "Someone needs to drive Halle's car, we shouldn't leave it here."

Matt volunteered. "I need keys."

"Did you check the car?" Jenna asked.

Matt pulled on the handle. "Locked."

Jenna reached into the back seat and searched Halle's pockets, quickly locating them.

"Here." She tossed them to Matt. "Call Lana. Let her know what's going on. I'm taking her to Lake Arella Memorial." Jenna called to Matt as he was getting into the driver's seat of Halle's SUV. "We'll meet you there." She turned her attention to Brandt. "Brandt, you getting in or what?" Jenna snapped. Brandt quickly complied.

On the way to the ER, Jenna had Brandt send a text to Levi and Jessica letting them know they wouldn't be back at The Glass House that night. Jenna fully expected them to all show up at the ER. Jessica couldn't resist drama.

They were five minutes away when Halle stirred and moaned quietly.

"I think she's coming around." Aedan kept his voice quiet, remembering how badly her head had hurt before. He swept a section of hair to the side that had fallen over Halle's cheek when she began to wake.

"My head." She groaned and nuzzled closer into the curve of Aedan's neck. "You smell good." She mumbled, still groggy.

A smug smile formed on Aedan's lips as Brandt glanced briefly over his shoulder at them.

"What did she say?" Jenna asked, taking a glimpse at Aedan in the rearview mirror.

Aedan's smile grew. "Apparently I smell good." He could see Jenna roll her eyes as the lights from a passing car lit her face.

"Mmm hmm." Halle moved her head slightly with the sound. "Aedan."

He tilted his head down to her, his lips resting dangerously close to the cheekbone by her ear and whispered, "Yes, Halle?"

"I dream about you." Her breath spilt

warmth on his neck when she spoke, sending a subtle tingling down his spine.

He continued to whisper, keeping the moment private. "And here I thought you didn't like me."

He felt the smile on her lips press against his collarbone as it turned up the corner of her mouth. "I don't like you," she said, burying her face further into the arc of his neck.

Jenna turned the car into the Emergency Room entrance.

"Good. I'm not right for you anyway." He brushed his lips against her cheek as he pulled his face away from hers and shifted her in his arms, preparing to exit the car when it stopped by the sliding doors. He closed his eyes for a brief moment, relishing the feel of Halle in his arms. He knew it wouldn't happen again. It couldn't.

When the car stopped, he rushed her into the busy emergency room. Lana was already waiting.

Almost three hours and countless cups of coffee later, a short bumbling man with round glasses and graying hair came into the waiting room where everyone sat or paced anxiously.

"Mrs. Michaels?" His mouth stretched into a smile when Lana stood.

"Yes?"

"I'm Dr. Hollowell. I treated Halle."

"How is she?" Lana's voice held concern and impatience. "Can I see her?"

He looked through the chart in his hand. "She's going to be fine. She's still a little groggy. We've run several tests and everything looks fine. The MRI and CT scans both look normal. We are a little concerned about her eyesight. There are some ocular abnormalities consistent with Flash Burns, which may have been caused by the transformer explosion her friends think occurred. We'd like to keep her until she is fully conscious and able to talk to us about what she can or can't see."

Lana listened intently until he was done speaking. "Can I see her?"

"Of course. I'll have one of the nurses come out and take you to her room." He turned and disappeared back through the double doors he had entered from.

Lana walked over to the group of friends waiting. "She's going to be staying the night, guys. She's ok, but they want to keep her for observation." Lana didn't want to go into detail and then have to answer questions she wasn't sure about herself yet. "I appreciate you all staying and being such good friends, but there isn't anything you can do right now. Go home and get some rest. I'll have Jenna let you all know how she is tomorrow."

The nurse called Lana's name from an open door.

"Ms. M?" Jenna said, making her way to speak to Lana. "I'm going to stay here tonight if that's okay with you."

Lana smiled at her, placing a hand on her arm. "I expected no different dear." Lana turned to follow the nurse down the corridor.

Chapter Twelve

Jenna was pacing the length of the waiting room and back when Matt and Aedan returned from picking up Matt's Jeep from the club.

"No word?" Matt asked, stopping by the double doors to look down the hallway.

"No. Nothing." Jenna replied.

Aedan took a seat in the corner and picked up a magazine from the table. He was beginning to feel the effects of being in physical form. Sapphira had warned him these bodies needed daily rest, just like any other mortal. That was starting to make sense. Mortals needed sleep and food. He was feeling the need for both.

"I'm going to the cafeteria. You two want anything?" Matt was already standing by the open elevator door.

Jenna smiled. "Coffee, two sugars, one cream."

Aedan looked up from the magazine. "That sounds good, make that two."

Matt nodded and stepped into the elevator, the doors closing behind him.

Jenna stopped pacing and looked intently at Aedan until he acknowledged her stare.

"Something on your mind, Jenna?"

"Yeah." She walked toward him, but didn't sit down. Just stood looking down at him, her hands on her hips. "What's your angle?"

"I'm sorry, what?"

"Your angle. Your intentions." Her tone dropped as she crossed her arms over her chest. "What are you trying to accomplish here, Aedan?"

He had no clue how to answer; he went with the truth Sapphira had so clearly pointed out to him earlier. "I care about her. I just want to make sure she's safe."

Jenna eyed him warily. Something behind her gaze sent a shiver of caution to his core. She took a few steps and sat in a chair, leaving an empty one between them. "She's an amazing person. I understand why you're drawn to her. I really do."

He arched an eyebrow slightly. "But?"

Jenna smiled. "But . . . do you really think you're right for her? She's been hurt before. Pretty badly. His name was Camden. It's a long story, but I don't want to see that happen again. Even if you don't mean to do it, it would happen. Call it a gut feeling. Do you understand what I'm saying?"

One corner of his mouth turned up in a slight smile. "She's very lucky to have a friend like you."

An immediate look of surprise spread over Jenna's face. She was a bit taken back. "Like me? What do you mean, like me?"

Afraid he'd hit a nerve, he tried to recover. "Protective." His tone was reassuring. "Not too many friends would be so concerned with such things."

"I'm very concerned about Halle," she said, turning her face solemnly in the direction of the patient wing. Had anyone known the secrets she knew about Halle, the statement would have held more meaning. Now that she knew about Halle's dreams as well as the voices, her concern grew. Jenna wondered if another dream had taken Halle to the warehouse district and she hadn't told anyone why she was there, just like the park.

"That's understandable." Aedan replied. "She seems to have a penchant for getting herself into dangerous situations."

Jenna turned back toward him.

He continued. "First the park. Now this. Is she always such a magnet for excitement?"

"Not until the last few weeks, really." Jenna's smile was strained. She opened her mouth to say something but was cut short by the sound of the elevator. Matt stepped off with a drink tray in one hand and a white paper bag in the other.

He lifted the drink tray slightly. "Coffee." He smiled, then lifted the bag. "And pastries. I was starved the moment the scent of muffins hit me. Thought you guys might be too."

Aedan gladly accepted one of the blueberry muffins.

"They aren't as good as Ms. M's pastries and baked goods, but they'll do in a pinch." Matt handed the last one to Jenna.

"Did you already eat one?" She smiled at him.

"Maybe." Matt winked at her and handed her a coffee before taking the seat beside her. "I wonder why this is taking so long."

"The doctor said something about Halle's eyesight." Jenna took a sip of coffee between sentences. "I was trying to read his lips when he was talking to Ms. M."

"What about it?" Matt asked.

"I don't know. He just said they were concerned."

They sat in silence for another twenty minutes, reading magazines or watching the news playing on the TV in the corner, until Lana pushed through the door leading to the patient wing. Their attention immediately turned to her.

"How is she?" Jenna asked first, almost jumping to her feet.

"She seems fine, except, she can't see. At all."

Jenna asked what they were all wondering. "Is it permanent?"

Lana was clearly fighting back tears, trying to stay strong. "They can't say for sure, but they are trying to be positive, I can tell. They think it should heal itself in three or four days. I'm just going to pray they are right."

Jenna walked over to Lana. "I'm sure they are." She hugged her tightly. "Can we go see her?"

"Actually, she asked if you all were still here. She doesn't remember a lot of what happened, but she clearly remembers who brought her in." Lana flashed a knowing smile at Aedan. "She wants to see you guys, but I have a question first. Aedan, Matt told me you had Philip trace Halle's phone to find her. Can he trace where the text message she got came from too? Because, I didn't send it and I want to know who put my baby in harm's way."

"I'll ask." He replied, wanting nothing more

than to know for sure who had lured Halle to the warehouse.

"Thank you. Come on. She's awake for now anyway." Lana walked back toward the door by the nurses' station.

Halle was sitting up in the hospital bed, eyes closed, when Jenna pushed the door open slowly. The room was dark to avoid strain on Halle's eyes. The only light came from the nightlights in the baseboards.

"Hey Jen."

Jenna shoved the door the rest of the way. "How'd you know it was me?"

"You're perfume. You smell like a mix of Eternity and oranges. Have you been eating oranges?" She smiled, her eyes now open, and focused straight ahead. She didn't turn her head in Jenna's direction until Jenna spoke.

"You know I don't eat oranges." She sat down in the chair by Halle's bed.

Halle's forehead crinkled as if she were confused. She inhaled slowly. "Aedan? Is he with you?"

"He's in the hall with Matt. Why?"

Halle smiled. "Just thought he might be,

that's all."

She could almost hear the corners of Jenna's mouth turn up as she spoke. "Yeah. I hear he smells pretty good."

"What?" Halle tilted her head.

Jenna laughed. "You don't remember saying that to him in the car, huh?" She was still laughing.

"I did what?" Halle sounded horrified.

"Oh yeah. In your half-conscious stupor, you told dreamy guy he smelled good."

Halle buried her face in both hands. "Oh. My. God. No I didn't."

"Oh yes. Yes, you did."

"I'm afraid to ask what else I may have said."

A knock on the door broke the conversation. It squeaked open and Matt stuck his head in. "Hey, Hal. Am I interrupting girl talk?"

"Since when did it matter?" Jenna jabbed at him.

"Come on in." Halle said, reaching for the blanket she felt lying over her feet at the end of the bed. "Can someone hand me that? It's a little chilly in here."

Instead of handing it to her, someone pulled it up over her, tucking it in around her waist. His fingers lingered over her skin as he brushed against her hand in the process. The electric surge of his touch would have given him away even if his scent hadn't.

"Thank you, Aedan." Halle all but whispered, her teeth tugging on her bottom lip. A habit Aedan had come to recognize as a warning sign. She was either thinking very hard about something or nervous. Either way, something stirred inside him every time she did that.

"You're welcome. How are you feeling?"

"I feel pretty drained, to be honest. And the not being able to see anything is kind of unnerving. Other than that, I'm fine."

Jenna piped in. "Your mom told us the doc said it was temporary."

"Yeah. I know, but there's always a chance it isn't. I heard them talking in the hallway. Guess we'll know in a few days, huh? Until then, it's strange to rely so much on your other senses."

"You mean like that super sniffer of yours?" Jenna poked Halle's arm with her finger and looked at Aedan and grinned. "I guess we will all have to make sure we smell good for the next few days."

Halle pulled a hand up to cover her face in embarrassment.

Matt had been friends with the girls long enough to know he was out of the loop. "Did I miss something?"

Jenna leaned toward him and whispered, "I'll explain it later."

"Jen, Mom said you were planning to stay. You don't have to do that. They're going to let me go home first thing in the morning. Just be at my house when I get there, okay?"

"You sure? I really don't mind staying. I don't want you to be by yourself."

"Yeah. I'm just going to sleep anyway. Not like we can stay up watching TV. And besides, I'm pretty exhausted. I don't remember what happened, but it really took it out of me."

"Okay. Well, I guess we'll get going then. So you can rest."

Halle stopped them. "Wait."

"What's up, Hal?" Matt grabbed her hand.

She squeezed it when he did. "Thank you. Ya'll are the best friends anyone could ask for."

"It's a three way street, Hal." Matt squeezed back on her hand.

"Love you guys." Halle smiled. She knew they smiled too, even though she couldn't see it, she just knew.

Matt and Jenna both hugged her and started to leave. Aedan was following them to the door when he told Halle goodbye.

"I hope you get to feeling better."

"Aedan, wait a sec."

"Yes?" He stood with the door propped open with one hand.

"Can I talk to you a minute?"

"Of course. What's up?" He walked back to the bedside and sat in the chair Jenna had occupied moments earlier.

"Well. I know I wasn't very nice in the park when we met and I feel like I owe you an apology for that. So, I'm sorry. You seem to be rescuing me a lot lately and I, just, well. Thank you."

The awkward silence was more than Halle could stand. Was he amused at her apology, ticked at the reminder of her attitude? She wanted desperately to be able to see his expression. Not being able to see his reaction made the blindness even more unsettling. It was only a matter of seconds, but it seemed like so much more.

"Halle." When he spoke, his voice held something she couldn't put her finger on. Even her name sounded safe when he said it. "You don't have to thank me. But please stop putting yourself in situations that could get you hurt, or worse. I don't want you to get hurt."

She smiled. "Fair enough. I'll see what I can do about that."

"I'll let you rest now."

She heard him stand to leave. "Would you mind staying until I fall asleep? Mom went home; I told her I was going to let Jenna stay because I didn't want her here worrying. I thought I wanted to be alone, but truth is – I'd feel better if someone were here."

He knew he wasn't leaving that night regardless. Whether he was there physically or not, he was staying. "Of course. Can I get you something? They have pretty decent muffins in the cafeteria."

She smiled. Aedan was convinced the room got brighter when she did.

"No, thanks. To be honest, I feel like I went Mach 20 and my stomach still hasn't recovered."

Aedan smirked at her comparison. She didn't realize how accurate her assessment was. It was likely closer to Mach 25, but she had the overall understanding.

"So, tell me about y –"

The nurse walked in before Halle could finish her sentence.

"Hello again, Ms. Halle."

"Hi, Ms. Shirley."

"I'm just here to check your vitals one last time before my shift is over and give you something to help you sleep." The bubbly nurse sat the small cup with two tiny pills by Halle's bed with a cup of water and proceeded to check her blood pressure and heart rate.

She pursed her lips as she held the stethoscope to the pulse point on Halle's arm. Her heart rate was off the charts. "Hmm." Shirley glanced over at Aedan sitting in the chair and smiled.

"Everything okay, Ms. Shirley?" Halle heard the sound she'd made.

Shirley patted her hand. "You are perfectly normal dear. Perfectly normal." She smiled brightly as she handed Halle the cup of water and held her hand while she placed the pills in her palm. "Okay. You're all set. You have a good night sweetie. Get better soon."

"Thanks, Ms. Shirley. Good night."

Shirley grinned at Aedan as she left the room.

Halle felt around for the side table to sit the empty cup down. "Now what were we talking about?"

Aedan took the cup from her and sat it on the table. "We weren't yet. Tell me about you."

"What about me?" she asked.

"Anything. Everything. Tell me about your family." He wanted to know what made Halle the person she was. The seemingly fearless, caring young woman who put her life in danger to try to help people she didn't even know. The person who brought him out of the darkest period of his existence into a place that he actually felt something again. He wanted to know who she was on a level no one else knew.

Halle was in the middle of telling Aedan

about her Nana Lisleigh and her last visit to Ireland when the sleeping pills kicked in.

Aedan took comfort in watching her sleep. It was a far cry from the feeling of helplessness he'd suffered only hours earlier as she fought for her life.

After several minutes, a familiar voice severed the silence.

"I was wondering when one of you would crash out or if I was going to have to listen to you two girls gossip about boys and braid each other's hair all night."

Aedan shook his head and chuckled to himself. "What are you doing here, Jess?"

"I'm here for Halle duty. You, sir, are being summoned to the great hall for the briefing of the D." He bowed as though he were in sixteenth century Europe.

Still laughing quietly at Jess, Aedan stood and stretched. "You really need to get out more, you know that?"

Jess nodded in agreement.

"If anyone undesirable shows up . . . call me."

Jess raised a mocking eyebrow. "By undesirable, do you mean Apollo-ish or that hunky football player who took her to dinner last week and sent her flowers?"

A sly smile turned up one corner of Aedan's

mouth. "Either." He traced out without another word.

Chapter Thirteen

By early Sunday morning, Halle was settling into her own bed. Doctor's orders, dark room with lots of rest until her eyesight healed. Could be a day, could be up to two weeks. There was no set schedule for Flash Burns to the optical nerves.

"Mom, you can go to church. I'll be fine. I'm just going to sit here with my iPod listening to Third Day so I don't totally miss the whole church experience."

Lana rolled her eyes at Halle and sighed while rearranging a few things to make sure nothing was in Halle's path between the bed and the bathroom.

"I heard that." Halle joked. "Don't roll your eyes at me. Just go to church."

"I don't want to leave you here alone in case you need something." Lana fluffed a pillow and placed it behind Halle.

"Mom, Jen is coming over in like ten minutes, remember? I'll be fine for two hours."

"I —" Lana tried to protest again.

"Jesus would want you to be in church." Halle had been waiting years to be able to use that line after hearing it from Lana on numerous occasions. She smiled, satisfied with herself.

"Cute, young lady. But true."

Halle's smile widened.

"Fine, I'll see you after church. Call if you need anything. Use the voice command." She placed the phone in Halle's hand.

"Yes ma'am. Love you."

"Love you too." Lana kissed Halle's forehead and left.

The door shutting downstairs and Lana's car pulling out of the driveway echoed as if she'd been standing right beside both.

It was insane how intensified her hearing and sense of smell had become. Even her sense of taste and touch were heightened. When the door knob downstairs turned, she focused on the sound, listening as Jenna's footsteps padded across the kitchen floor. By the time she reached the bottom of the stairs the scent of oranges and faint hint of perfume swept over her.

"Jenna!" Halle called to her before her foot hit the first step. "Bring me a cream soda please!"

"Got it." Jenna replied and arrived in Halle's room minutes later, two cream sodas in hand. "So, what do you want to do? Not that you have a lot of options."

Halle smiled. "I want to figure a few things out."

"Like what? World peace?" Jenna twisted the top from one of the bottles and placed it in Halle's already outstretched hand. "I have a few ideas on that."

"Maybe after, first I want you to bring me things and not tell me what you're handing me. It's an experiment. I want to see just how in tune my other senses have become since I can't use one of them."

Jenna wasn't sure the reason for Halle's fascination, but it was better than sitting and listening to music or ranting about school and whatnot. "So, is this just for touch? Or am I going to make noises and bring things for you to smell and taste too?"

Halle shrugged. "Maybe all of it. I just think it's kind of crazy how well I'm hearing and smelling things now."

"Okay then." Jenna played along. First she brought a few objects for Halle to guess what they were using touch. Then she padded to different areas of the house as quietly as possible and waited for Halle to tell her what room she was in. It got a little eerie when Halle called Jenna out for stopping in the kitchen and quietly taking a bite of a cookie from a plate sitting on the counter.

"You better bring me one of those cookies you're eating." Halle yelled to her.

"Are you serious?" Jenna called back.

"Uhh, yes. I want a cookie."

Jenna trotted back up the stairs, cookie in hand. "Okay, Hal, there is no way you heard me eat a cookie."

"Eerie, huh?" Halle smiled and held her hand out, wiggling her fingers for the cookie. "I believe it is chocolate chip macadamia nut?"

"You're a little creepy." Jenna said, placing the cookie in her hand. "Let's see what else you've got."

Jenna looked around. The angel on the dresser caught her attention. She picked it up and plopped down on the bed at Halle's feet.

"Alright, I'm not giving you this object. I'm only going to let you touch parts of it and see if you can guess what it is. Okay?"

Halle shook her head in agreement.

"Hold your hand out."

Halle did as instructed. Jenna turned the

angel upside down and only let Halle run her fingers across the bottom of the wooden base. It was flat and glossed over. Jenna thought maybe she wouldn't pick up on the material.

After a few circular motions Halle stopped the movement and lifted all fingers but one from the surface. She then continued to slowly glide her middle finger across the finish. After two passes she made a rectangular shape over and over then stopped and lifted her last finger.

"Whatever it is, it must have batteries in it." She said, confident of her finding.

Jenna looked at her confused. "It doesn't have batteries, why would you say that?"

"Because it has a battery compartment." Halle reached her hand back toward the object. "It's right here." She traced a finger around the edges of the rectangle again. A rectangle Jenna couldn't see.

"Hal. There's nothing there. This is the bottom of the angel your dad gave you." Her voice quivered with hesitation.

"What? That can't be right. I've handled that thing a thousand times. I've never felt or seen anything on the bottom other than the inscription." She took the angel from Jenna's hands and began running her finger over it again.

"Right here, don't you feel it?" She held it for Jenna to touch.

"It feels smooth to me."

Halle sat the angel in her lap and proceeded to run the one finger lightly over every part of the porcelain figure. She stopped when her finger glided over something she hadn't paid any attention to before. The angel wore a cross around his neck.

"Can you see this?" She asked Jenna, pointing to the cross.

"Yes. It's a cross. Why?"

"I've just never noticed it before. I know there is one engraved in the wood on the front of the base."

"Yeah. It actually looks just like that one." Jenna told her.

Halle moved her fingers down to the cross carved into the wood of the base. She studied it with her touch and tilted her head then stopped.

"What is it?" Jenna knew that look. It was the look of discovery.

"I think it comes off." She said, trying to get a grip to pull on the carving, but as she tried to pull, it turned in place a little instead. "Well, either this thing is supposed to move or I just broke it." Halle placed one hand under the base for support and tightened her grasp on the cross before she turned it clockwise as if she were winding it up. Something clicked inside and so she turned it once more.

Another click.

She tilted her head toward Jenna. "Third time's a charm?"

Jenna was speechless.

Halle twisted the cross once more, releasing another clicking sound – and the rectangular piece in the base. Something fell into her hand. She wrapped her palm around it and sat the angel to the side, rolling the object between her fingertips. A necklace. A cross necklace.

"Jen, look at this."

"I am. I'm just not believing it."

Halle was a little blown away too. "It's a cross, right?"

"Yeah."

"The circle shape in the middle threw me off a little. I wish I could see it." She continued to caress it between her fingertips, studying its form. "What's this on the back of it?" She turned it over and showed it to Jenna. "I can feel the shape, but it isn't something I'm familiar with. Do you recognize it?"

Jenna was silent for a moment.

"Jen?"

"Yeah. Yeah, I recognize it. I've seen it on something at church. It looks like a cross between an omega, an angel, and a tribal tattoo you'd get to piss your mom off. I guess it's some kind of symbol for something."

"Do you think this is what the inscription in the base of the angel is about?" Halle tried to remember what it Toby had said it translated into. "My purse. The paper is still in my purse. Find it."

Jenna scrambled from the bed, still in shock and rummaged through Halle's purse for a minute. "Here. Here it is." She handed it to Halle without thinking.

Halle cleared her throat and waited for Jenna to realize the problem with that.

"Oh, right. Sorry." She opened the paper and read the inscription's meaning from the print off Toby had sent. "Appearances are deceptive. Look inside for the key to dreams."

Jenna sat stunned, reading the phrase again and again silently. There had to be more to it.

Halle brought her out of the thought cycle. "How would this necklace be the key to dreams?" A confused chuckle. "That just doesn't make any sense."

"Maybe it does." Jenna's tone came across vaguely ambiguous. "Halle?"

"Yeah?"

"Where's the book Uncle T sent you?"

Halle thought a few seconds. "Well, the last I remember having it, I slid it under the bed. Check there. Why?"

Jenna hit the floor and peeked under the

bed. It was there. She pulled the box out and laid it on the bed. "I think it's the same shape as that groove in the top of your book."

She pulled the book out and asked Halle for the necklace.

"Well?" Halle asked. "I can't see it, I can hear that you're trying to make it fit, but you're going to have to give me the play by play."

Jenna placed it in the groove. It was the same shape, precisely. It wouldn't fit though.

"It is the right shape exactly, there's something on the back that won't let it lay flat in there."

"Did you think it was the key to the book?" Halle wasn't sure what Jenna was thinking might have been the outcome.

"Yeah, I guess I thought it was possible. Since your dad used to write in a journal and you write in a journal, I just thought maybe because you might write your dreams in it, it would be the key to dreams. I know. Crazy." Jenna handed the key back to Halle.

Halle fumbled it in her fingers for a few moments and stopped, her brows furrowed slightly. "Did you try turning it over?" Halle handed it back to Jenna.

"Hmm. Okay." She placed it upside down in the cross shaped opening. It locked into place.

Halle heard the connection. The way the

two metals fit perfectly together. "It works, doesn't it?" A satisfied smile formed on her lips.

"I think it does. Hold on." Jenna placed her fingers on the larger cross that the necklace nested into and turned it. Success.

"Wow, that is just... wow." Jenna mumbled. "Dangit!"

Halle's shriek caught Jenna off guard. She jumped a little.

"What?"

"I just wish I could see it. I wasn't really having an issue with the eyesight thing until right now. Suddenly, my patience is thin." Halle blew out a frustrated breath.

"You'll see it soon. You have to get your sight back by Friday, at the latest. That's an order." Jenna smiled.

"I know, I know. Or you're dragging me to the masquerade thing even if I can't see, right?"

"Yep. It'll be dark, won't bother your eyes."

"Okay, let's do something to keep my mind occupied because now I'm getting a little antsy." Halle fell back flat on the bed.

"Wellllll." Jenna drug the word out. "If your necklace here," she placed it in Halle's palm, "is any indication of Latin phrases meaning something; wouldn't you say it's possible the other phrases mean something too?"

Halle puckered her lips in a thinking gesture. "Maybe. After all, the angel and the book are now clearly connected." Halle quickly sat back up on the bed, recharged. "Read those translations to me again."

Jenna read them all.

"We need a Bible." Halle felt over to the nightstand by her bed and opened the top drawer. Seconds later she held a tattered Bible out to Jenna. "Here."

One by one, Jenna looked up the verses associated with each of the phrases.

"That doesn't really seem to help. They really just kind of mean the same thing the phrases mean." Her tone was discouraged.

Jenna perked up. "What was it you said in the car the other day, about what order they were in?"

"You weren't reading them in order just now?" Halle laughed.

"Well, I read them in the order they were written down."

"Let's put them in the order the verses are found in the Bible. That wouldn't change over time, remember?"

Jenna flipped to the Table of Contents and wrote the number beside each phrase that correlated with its place in the Bible. "Okay. Done."

"Yeah, still can't see." Halle quipped. "Read

it please?"

Jenna scrunched her nose. "Sorry. Let's see. One book leads to another, yet they are the same. I call the living, I mourn the dead. Begin here. In the presence of the people, within a place for repentance. Faith is to believe what you do not see; the reward of this faith is to see what you believe. At the threshold of the Apostles, lift your faces to the Light. The appearances of things are deceptive. From the cross, that which is hidden shall be revealed. The one who dreams holds the key."

"Yeah. Still cryptic." Halle tilted her head, listening. "Did you hear that?"

Jenna listened. "No. What?"

"I thought I heard someone say my name, but it wasn't in the house. Like it was coming from outside." Halle sat still for a moment, listening.

Jenna walked to the window and scanned the drive-way and yard. "No one there, Hal."

"Anyway. Whatever" Halle sighed.

Jenna sat back down on the bed. "Let's add the verses in with the phrases and see if it helps." Paper rattled as Jenna began flipping through the book, looking up the verses and writing them down. When she reached Mark 9:23 she found something tucked between the pages.

"Hal, what's this?"

"Describe, please."

"It's a piece of torn white fabric. Very soft, almost iridescent white fabric. It was in your Bible. Right here at one of the verses I was looking for."

Halle's expression must've alerted Jenna it was more than just a bookmark.

"Does it mean something?" Jenna moved it between her fingers. "It's really soft."

Halle held her palm out and Jenna placed it gently in her hand. The shock hit her again. It didn't send her flying off balance this time, but the images flashed through her mind again. Instinctively she closed her eyes. When she opened them, for a brief moment, she saw shadows and shapes in her room, but then they faded back to black.

"Halle? Does it mean something?" Jenna repeated the question.

"N-. No. Just holding a place in my Bible. What page was it on?"

"Mark chapter 9. One of the verses from the journal. Mark 9:23. The one about seeing what you believe."

"Here, just put it back for now." She handed it back to Jenna and wondered if it had the same effect on her when she touched it. And if it didn't, why not?

Jenna took it and watched Halle's expression knowing she continued to contemplate something. She completed adding all the verses to the phrases and then read over them to Halle a few times. The phrase about where to begin kept replaying in her mind.

"I don't know, Jen. It could be any church, anywhere that you're supposed to 'begin' at. Ya know."

"Yeah. Oh well. Not like we were going to go on some treasure hunt. Who knows what it leads to anyhow."

"Mom's home." Halle reached her hand for the journal and plucked the necklace from its resting place. It was another forty-five seconds before Lana pulled in the driveway.

"You heard her car that far down the road?" Halle shook her head.

"That is insane." Jenna was stunned. She placed the book in the box and slid it back under the bed. "I have to go work on that history assignment for a bit. You going to be okay until Matt gets here?"

Halle laughed. "I'll be fine. I'm not terminal. But would you help me put this on before you leave?" She held the necklace out.

"Sure thing." Jenna hooked the clasp while Halle held her hair out of the way. "I'll come back later this afternoon, m'kay?"

"No prob. Have fun with history."

"No doubt. Fun, fun." Jenna passed Lana on the stairs as she was leaving. "Watch out for her, she's developed bionic hearing since she can't see anything."

Lana laughed and said goodbye to Jenna.

Halle spent the next few days resting more than she felt was humanly possible and playing with her heightened senses. Matt and Jenna had come over every day to keep her company and give her the latest on what was going on at school. Sapphira and Philip brought her some puzzles made especially for the blind, it was thoughtful and something for Jenna to give her grief about at the same time.

Levi, Jessica and Brandt stopped by to visit on Wednesday. Brandt's visit was a little awkward and wasn't made any less so when Aedan showing up shortly after Brandt had arrived. It was almost as though his timing were impeccably planned to run Brandt off. Halle could feel the hostility thick in the air when the two were in the room simultaneously. The testosterone battle almost made her laugh. When Brandt left, Aedan fell back into the chair in the corner. *His chair*, Halle thought.

"So, chair guy." She laughed at her own

inside joke. "Long time no see." She laughed harder. He couldn't help but laugh with her.

"You're really making the best of this Helen Keller period, aren't you?" He smiled. Halle heard it, and realized she hadn't really seen him smile outside of dreams. And she had dreamt of the smile that promised something she ached for. Every night. Her heart lightened at the thought.

"The way I see it, I always have two choices. I choose to never let my nightmares get the better of me."

Aedan didn't stay long. He told Halle he had only come by to see how she was doing and that he needed to get back to the city. He tried not to offer too many details about his cover that he'd have to remember for later. He left, taking the crisp scent of rain with him.

By Thursday, she was seeing shapes and outlines mixed in with some beyond blurry color. But she was at least seeing something. That was what mattered. It was proof that the damage wasn't permanent. She still had to see the doctor Friday afternoon for a few more tests and to be released back into the wild, as Jenna had put it. She was really looking forward to being back among the living. Her room was great, but nothing like the wild.

Chapter Fourteen

When Friday morning rolled around, Halle would have paid someone to let her go to school. Not something she expected. Being cooped up in her house for five days hadn't been her idea of the most fun way to spend her first official week as an adult.

"Please, Mom." Her voice came out like a whining thirteen year old who was begging to go to a boy-girl party for the first time. "I'm fine. I can see everything." Which was true, even if it was as blurry as a Monet painting up close. "I just want to go to school. You can pick me up after lunch and take me to my appointment with Dr. Hollowell. Please."

Lana laughed. "I would have never thought

I'd hear you begging to go to school. I used to have to drag you out of bed some mornings."

"Exactly, so it would be a travesty to deny me this then. Give in to the irony, Mom." She kept following Lana around the kitchen, waiting for her to cave.

"I don't know, Hal."

"I'll wear sunglasses. Won't take them off until the doc says I can."

Lana stopped sliding files into her briefcase. She knew she would have to let Halle back out of the house at some point. Not knowing who had sent that text to Halle, or why, crept into her mind every time the thought of Halle being alone popped up. She looked at her daughter, face turned upward, eyes wide with childlike expression, pleading . . . for school of all places. She laughed. "Fine. Go to school."

"Yes!" Halle sprung from her position and wrapped her arms around her mother's neck. "Thank you, thank you, thank you."

Lana pulled back and pointed a motherly finger at her. "But keep the sunglasses on and I'll pick you up at 1:30. Your appointment's at 2:15."

"I know. Thank you, Mom."

"You're welcome." Lana responded as Halle bounced up the stairs, calling Jenna as she went.

Aedan had been keeping his distance all week. Darius assured him Halle was more than safe in her room, which she had mainly been in since coming home from the hospital. Sapphira was happily keeping watch over the Michael's home.

He used the time to regroup and refocus. Sparring with Darius and Jess had been high on the list. After the encounter with the shadow demon in the alley, he felt like it might be a good idea to get back into a warrior mindset. Having bursts of lux dei hurled at your head and dodging the brutal swiftness of Jess' sword was enough to bring out the most lethal of instincts.

After hours of hand to hand sparring and a little real life lux dei target practice, Jess' swift sword appeared almost from thin air.

"I was beginning to wonder if you were going soft." A slash of Jess' blade whipped by Aedan's arm – close enough that he reactively sidestepped to avoid contact.

Twisting away, he unsheathed his weapon. "Me? Soft? In your dreams."

Jess was a blur. "Maybe not mine, but I'd bet in hers, you are quite the pillow, aren't you?" Swords clashed as Aedan read his movement and met his attack as metal met metal.

"You shall never know." He pushed Jess away with the force of sword on sword.

"I could always visit her dream myself." Jess readied his stance. "Maybe she has a weakness for all Guardians."

Aedan swiped his blade impossibly fast, stopping it a hair shy of Jess' neck. "You do like to live dangerously, don't you?"

A slow smile crawled across Jess' face. "If it involves danger, I'm there. You, however, are playing with a fire out of my league, my friend."

Aedan removed the blade from Jess' throat and stepped away, Jess' words weighing heavy. "That's enough for now. I need to check in with Darius." He turned and left.

When the lunch bell rang, Halle sat in study hall a few minutes longer than everyone else, giving the crowd in the hallway time to thin out. Jenna took their books to the locker while Halle waited for her there. With her elbows resting on the desk, she ran her hands tightly into her hair and rested her forehead in her palms. Maybe coming to school today wasn't the best idea. Her senses were still off the charts and every smell, every sound, rocked her like a ten on the Richter scale. And the voices. It had been so quiet at home; she had started to forget about them. Walking through the front doors was a kick to the gut. There had to be a way to turn it all off. So much chatter, such putrid aromas mixed with such lovely ones. Much like the voices, it was almost impossible to separate the scents. She closed her eyes and tried to concentrate on blocking it all out.

"Halle?" The masculine voice was soft and quiet, like he was trying not to disturb her.

"Hi Brandt." She responded without looking up. The sense of hearing also made it easier to make out tones and subtle inflections that distinguished one voice from another. She lifted her head to meet his stare.

"Nice shades." He smiled and took a seat at the desk beside her. "Look, I know this is a little forward, and you've had a lot going on this week, but . . ." He was fumbling with his words again. Who was this guy? Certainly not the Brandt Lucas she was expecting.

"But what?" She asked point blank. Not in the mood for beating around the bush.

"Are you and the Aedan guy dating?" There it was. No sugar coating.

Halle laughed. "What?" She could honestly say, "No." Not that she didn't think about him, dream about him, wish he would ask her out, but, "No." Yeah. She'd already said that.

"Okay."

"Why would you think that?" Curiosity was known to kill the cat.

"Well, the other night, he was very possessive and protective. Wouldn't let anyone near you, and . . ."

Halle waited for the words following, "And what?"

"He did mention something about tucking you in. Let's just say he acted very much like, well, like I would if you were my girlfriend." A dangerously charming smile emerged, highlighting dimples that were known to make the female population swoon. Halle had no clue why his charms didn't have the same effect on her. Instead of getting lost in his come-hither eyes, her first thought was *Aedan tucked me in?* She was still thinking about Aedan when Brandt asked if she would be at Levi's big bash.

"Huh? Oh, tomorrow night? Yeah. Even if I didn't really want to go, I wouldn't have a choice. Jenna would drag me to it, blind or not. Wouldn't you?" Halle caught a trace of Jenna's orange blossom scent before she'd ever stepped fully into the room. Her scent seemed to be stronger than most. Probably because it was so familiar and easier to recognize.

"Yes. Yes I would." Jenna had no qualms in

dragging Halle, even if she kicked and screamed. "You will be there, won't you Brandt?"

"Absolutely." He smiled. "I'm hoping to have a dance or twenty with Halle, if she'll let me."

"I'm sure that could be arranged. Right, Halle?" Jenna was relentless.

"Don't I need to be able to see, so I don't step on toes?" She joked, but meant it.

"So what will you be wearing?" Brandt directed the question at Halle.

"Now, if I tell you, doesn't that ruin the point of a *Masquerade*?" Her own teasing smile emerged.

"Then I shall spend the evening searching for you if I must." He flashed his million dollar smile again and headed for the door. "I'll see you both tomorrow night."

"I don't think I can take the nauseating blend of rancid cafeteria food and God knows what else in the lunchroom today. I hope this super sniffer fades when my eyesight is back to normal. Otherwise, I may never eat again."

Jenna laughed.

"What? It's really not funny. Really."

"Not what I was laughing at."

"Okay, what were you laughing at then?"

"You." Blunt. To the point. Classic Jenna. "I just don't get you, Halle Michaels."

"What's not to get? I don't like the rotten

smell of cafeteria food."

"I meant Brandt. The hottest guy in school just walked out of here, after flirting mercilessly with you and your first comment was about cafeteria food. Should I be questioning which team you're batting for? Because you're my best friend, no matter what, but seriously. Brandt Lucas. Hello."

Halle inhaled and blew out a deep breath. "Well...there is something about him, something that definitely keeps me off balance around him. But he just doesn't make the butterflies whip around like they're on crack. Ya know?"

Jenna raised a finger to her mouth in thought. "Nothing? At all?"

"Don't get me wrong. He's definitely a ten on the Jenna scale. But, he doesn't make my pulse race or my heart do that beat skipping thing. Isn't that what we are all waiting for? Why should I waste my time on anything less?"

Jenna didn't know what to say.

Halle grabbed her purse hanging from the back of her chair. "C'mon. You're driving me to Murphy's for a burger. I'm buying."

"If you're buying I'm driving, but you're springing for a mint chocolate chip shake too then."

"Done." Anything to get out of the sensory overload zone.

Murphy's, the small diner with the best bacon cheeseburgers in Lake Arella, was packed as always. Jenna snagged a small booth just as a couple was sliding out to leave.

"You know we aren't going to make it back in time for third period, right?"

Halle looked at a pretend watch. "We have forty-five minutes. We'll be fine."

She wore the sunglasses like she'd promised Lana, even though it was fairly overcast. Strangely enough, Halle could smell the clouds hanging low and dark in the sky, threatening to open up at any moment. It wasn't the smell of rain. It was different somehow. The electricity in the air pressed against her skin too, but something else pushed at her senses. Something more menacing than the threat of any storm. An unshakable gut feeling that she was being watched wouldn't go away.

"Jen, I know this is going to sound paranoid, but I feel like someone's watching us. Anyone seem creepy around here? I can't see well enough to check everyone out."

Jenna glanced around the room. "Just a bunch of typical lunch crowd types. Not seeing anyone who screams 'let's jump Halle in a dark alley.'"

Halle's head tilted. "Why would you say that?"

Jenna tightened her lips together as she remembered that Lana hadn't told Halle that she didn't send the text about the warehouse. Which meant Halle's feeling of paranoia was coming from somewhere else. Maybe her heightened senses were messing with her head.

"I don't know, Hal. Sorry. That was a stupid thing to say."

When the waitress sat their plates in front of them Jenna tried to take the topic away from her foot in mouth act. "Mmm. This place smells great."

"It would if the aroma wasn't overpowered by whatever they've burnt in the kitchen."

"I don't smell anything burnt." Jenna squirted ketchup onto her plate and handed the bottle to Halle.

"How can you not smell that? I'm surprised the fire department isn't down here. It smells like they melted a hundred boxes of plastic spoons back there and topped it off with burnt meat. And I thought this was a non-smoking establishment." Halle squinted her nose and turned to sit the ketchup at the end of the table. For a split second the man two booths over was crystal clear while everything around him was a blur. She squeezed her eyes together and shook her head then looked again. The image was gone, faded back into the blur.

"Jen."

"Hmm?" She finished chewing her fry.

"Two booths over. There's a man sitting by himself. Do you see him?"

Jenna changed position to see to the booth. "No."

"He's wearing a black suit with a red shirt. No tie."

Jenna looked again. "Hal, the second booth down is empty. No plates, no person, no nothing." She paused. "Are you okay?"

"Yeah. Fine. I guess my eyes are just playing tricks on me. I'll be glad when I'm back up to speed." She brushed it off. "We should hurry. I don't want to miss art class."

"Or have the principal tell your mom you skipped."

"That too."

Chapter Fifteen

Dr. Hollowell gave strict instructions as Halle slid the sunglasses back on. No bright lights, so the Masquerade Ball was a go and Jenna would be giddy. No direct sun exposure for another week, meaning shades at school would be a fashion statement. Watching TV was a no-no. Clearly the DVR would be recording *Psych* and *White Collar* for yet another episode. And, obviously, driving was still not on the table.

"I'd say you'll be back to normal in another week." The roundness of Dr. Hollowell's face was accentuated by his smile. "Over the next day or two, things should start to clear up instead of being so blurry."

"Thank you." Lana shook his hand.

"My pleasure. You take care, Halle."

"I will try. Thank you." Halle was already hopping down from the examination table. "Can we go home now? I'm ready to veg out a little."

"Sure. I just need to stop by the cleaners before we leave town. Need to pick up your dress."

"My dress?"

"I had Nana Lisleigh's dress cleaned and pressed for you to wear tomorrow night."

"You didn't have to do that, but thank you."

"It had been in the attic for twenty years. Trust me, I had to."

"Jenna's going to want to start getting ready tomorrow at like nine a.m." Halle laughed. "I have never seen anyone so excited to go to a Masquerade Ball, and believe me – there are a lot of cheerleaders from school going."

Lana smiled. "You know, you should be a little excited too. These things are fun. Enjoy life while you can sweetheart. Play dress up. Step out of your comfort zone. Chase your dreams. Live."

Chase your dreams, Halle thought. What a concept. The last few dreams she had chased didn't end so well. She'd been slammed into a bathroom wall and tackled to the ground by a Greek god. Okay, so the last one could have been a lot worse. If she could choose which dreams to chase and which ones to toss into the abyss, that would be ideal. Sadly her dreams didn't seem to function that way.

"Speaking of Greek gods." Halle half whispered inadvertently as Lana pulled into the driveway.

"What dear?"

Halle shook her head without words. Her attention was focused on the figure in the yard next door. His image coming through clearly. She blinked and it blurred again.

"He is extremely handsome, isn't he?" Halle could hear the teasing approval in Lana's smile without looking.

"Handsome?" Halle asked in an understated tone.

"You're right. He looks like he should have been carved from marble. Is that better?"

"More accurate." She smiled. "He's flippin' gorgeous. I have yet to figure out why Jenna doesn't like him."

Lana put the car into Park and turned the ignition off. "Jenna hasn't been ooooing and ahhhing over him?" Disbelief hung in her words.

"No. And instead of encouraging me to think he's beautiful, she's all about some Brandt and me."

"Maybe she likes him but doesn't want to say anything."

"I don't think so. I could be wrong. But I

don't think that's it." Halle felt around for her purse in the blur of the floorboard.

"You're right. I keep expecting her and Matt to show up all googly-eyed over each other someday."

"You and half of LA High." Halle laughed. "They fight like they've been dating for years."

Lana opened the door and was fighting to get the oversized box from the back seat when Halle was enveloped in the scent of clean rain and crisp linen. "Aedan's coming, isn't he?"

Lana turned to see Aedan jogging across the lawn. "Let me help you with that Mrs. Michaels."

"Thank you, Aedan, that's very sweet of you." She let him maneuver the box from the back seat. "It's Halle's dress for tomorrow night. Not overly heavy, but awkward."

"Fairly heavy for a dress," he said, pushing the car door shut with his free hand.

"It's well made. Family heirloom. It was my mother's."

Halle was slowly making her way to the door when Lana moved past her. Aedan came up beside her and offered his arm in a courteous manner.

"Thank you," she said, lacing her arm through his, bracing for the electric charge his touch always activated. She didn't need his arm to guide her, but she wasn't about to pass on chivalry.

He leaned down closer to her and asked, "So, what did the doc say?"

"Apparently, I'm too stubborn to stay injured. I'm going to be fine. Just have to stay out of harsh or direct light for another week."

"So you're starting to get your sight back?" He looked down, catching her gaze.

"Slowly. But I can see shapes and shadows." *And cobalt eyes filled with secrets.* She wondered what might be hiding behind the endless sea of blue.

Halle walked through the door, expecting Aedan to follow. He stopped in the mudroom.

"I should get back. Sapphira is expecting me for dinner." He placed the box on top of the washing machine and turned to leave, then paused and looked back. "I'll see you later, Halle."

"Okay. Thanks for your help." Why did being around him tie her tongue and cause her brain to function at half caliber? She closed the door and headed to her room. It was going to be an early night.

Chapter Sixteen

That night, she dreamt she was standing alone, in an open field. The cover of darkness kept her from noticing the headstones scattered across the hill. She looked down to find she was wearing her Nana Lisleigh's red ball gown and in the distance, a bell chimed its eerie summoning. It begged her to go to it. It called to her. She started walking. She walked and walked, until she felt the presence of something familiar behind her. Something that hunted her. Had hunted her before. She ran.

When she woke, she was still gasping for air. Her heart was still pounding in her chest. She took several long, deep breaths, trying to steady her heart rate and calm her breathing. One last inhale caught her by surprise. Rain. And linen. "Aedan?"

The moment his name slipped from Halle's lips in the dark of her room, he traced out. Something in the tone of her voice told him she wasn't dreaming. His warrior instinct wasn't typically one to choose flight over fight, but Halle wasn't someone he was prepared to fight anyway. He wasn't sure what she was capable of.

What he didn't realize was that in his haste, he traced himself dead in the middle of a meeting between Darius and two of Marom's highest ranking angels.

"Aedan." Darius leaned back in his chair and glanced around, drawing attention to those in attendance.

He found himself the object of cold glares. Osiris and Bastian. Bastian was Osiris' equal only he answered to Michael, where Osiris answered to Gabriel. Aedan knew Bastian well; he had been his superior for ages when Aedan's duties fell under the title of Warrior.

"My apologies." A slow bow of the head and Aedan took a few steps toward the door leading out of the safe house's game room.

Bastian spoke. "Aedan, stay." It wasn't a request. It was an order.

Aedan turned on his heel. "If you wish."

"Please, have a seat. We are discussing your assignment." Osiris tended to come across in a more tranquil manner. The distinction between Guardian and Warrior, he assumed. A distinction Aedan remembered learning during his transfer.

"How can I be of assistance?" Aedan knew Bastian nor Osiris would be interested in anything more than the cold hard facts. Best to let them ask questions and simply answer.

Osiris began. "We know of the book. Both of them. There is a key that we know opens the book Ms. Michaels possesses."

"Halle has the key as well, Aedan. But that isn't all, I'm afraid." Darius was beyond formalities. Aedan had no doubt that Darius could easily be sitting in a position of command like the two beings before them, had he accepted the role when offered. Darius turned it down for reasons no one knew.

"What do you need me to do?" Aedan asked.

"We need the second book. She is the means to obtaining it." Bastian was no nonsense. Always had been. Mortals were disposable in his mind. A means to an end. He protected them when ordered to do so, but when it came down to a choice between Marom and humanity, there was no choice for Bastian. He was a Warrior. Defending Marom was his sole purpose.

"According to our sources, there are instructions that will lead to the Book of Dreams."

Aedan was too curious not to ask what Osiris was referring to. "Book of Dreams?"

"Noah Michaels was no ordinary mortal. He was a prophet. He was given information through dream sequences. He wrote this information into the book, the one that has been lost. Darius tells us that you have seen the replica. That Miss Michaels has it by some strange line of events. Our trackers have learned that Noah had the book put in place so that Halle would find it. The replica has the instructions. I believe the phrases you obtained from the book are the source of finding the Book of Dreams." Osiris looked to Darius, as though waiting for permission to continue.

Instead, Darius continued. "Gabriel has met with the Sanhedrin. When Noah died, Gabriel petitioned to have Halle continue his work when she came of age. They denied the request."

Aedan wasn't sure where this was going. He waited and listened, knowing there was more.

"They denied the request, because of her heritage." Darius' face appeared hollow and dark. "I'm afraid we are going to have to find a way to take Halle's book and her key. It isn't safe with her."

Aedan didn't fully understand, and knew he

wouldn't. The Sanhedrin's word was final. No questions asked.

"I am to assume I have orders then?" Aedan asked, his tone a blade of steel.

"For now, you are to continue on as her Guardian. We are waiting for orders to be approved, but if she does anything that might even hint to an allegiance with the Hellions, we need to kn —" Bastian cut Osiris short.

"Make no mistake, Aedan. It may come down to the need to take her out. Be prepared."

Aedan's eyes shot to Darius, seeking contradiction. What he got instead, was confirmation. Aedan offered a slow nod and retreated from the room.

This couldn't be right. Halle couldn't possibly be enough of a threat that she would warrant being eradicated. Someone, somewhere had to be wrong.

The sun was setting when Aedan received orders he wasn't sure he wanted. He was to retrieve the key from Halle by whatever means necessary.

"And the book?" he asked, his flat tone at odds with the storm of uncertainty raging inside.

"We will take care of that. You take care of the girl." Bastian's timbre was death sheathed in velvet. Aedan knew what the underlying meaning was. Let her die if necessary. It was a Warriors instinct to know that battle meant casualties.

"Aedan." Darius' voice linked quietly to him. *"We all care about her. But it seems your instincts were right all along. She isn't who we thought. I'm sorry."*

"As am I, Darius. I will get the key." Aedan closed the link and turned to Jess.

"Something isn't right here. Tell me everything you know. I don't care if it's been deemed to the highest security. Someone has a price on Halle's head and my gut tells me it has something to do with what she has the power to do to them."

Jess listened to all Aedan had to say about the meeting and the book. When they had finished exchanging information, both knew less about the truth of this assignment than before.

"Aedan, unofficial word on the street is that Nakita has been jumping the fence."

Aedan's head snapped around. "Nakita?"

"Yeah. She's been asking a lot of questions that are a little outside of her pay grade. Things trackers don't need to know."

Aedan paced a few steps as he ripped his

hand through his hair.

"I know that look. What is it?" Jess was certain wheels were turning in Aedan's head.

"That first night, at The Glass House. When I said I went to speak to an old friend."

Jess didn't wait for the name. "Nakita."

He shook his head to agree.

"I can't leave Halle unguarded, Jess. I don't think Apollo is the only one with a price on her head. How do you feel about masquerades?"

"Isn't that what we do every day?" Jess grinned. "Besides, I do love to dance."

Chapter Seventeen

"I can't believe you are wearing knee high boots with that dress." Jenna wouldn't let it go, the entire drive to Levi's house.

"If I'd have worn heels, the dress would be too short. I'm clearly taller than Nana Lisleigh. Besides, these are so much more comfy and no one can see them anyway."

Jenna rolled her eyes. "Okay, okay. Regardless, you look amazing. That is by far the most gorgeous dress ever. Believe me, I tried to find one that would even come close. I couldn't."

Halle smiled at Jenna. Her stunning purple dress was such a shade so deep it was almost black. The iridescent quality to the top layer really made it stand out. Plus, it worked great with Jenna's platinum blonde hair.

Halle had insisted they drive her SUV. They'd have never gotten both of those dresses into Jenna's VW Bug and Matt had gone over to Levi's early. He'd said to help Levi set up, but since Levi's brother Asa had hired people to handle everything, Halle was convinced it was just so he didn't have to listen to them go on and on about their hair and dresses.

The day had set cold and gray with a sky that seemed to be lowering by the minute. Dark, angry clouds loomed just beyond the hills to the west, a harbinger of worse to come.

"I hope the rain holds off." Jenna mumbled. "At least until we can get inside. Our hair does not need to be getting wet. I'm not so sure curls would survive a downpour." She turned into the long driveway that snaked its way to Levi's house. Halle's sight had improved more than she'd imagined in a short twenty-four hours. Anything within twenty or so feet was fairly clear. Beyond that could be a bit blurry or downright unrecognizable. Depending on the moment.

In the fading light of day, Levi's house held a haunting majesty. Intricate gothic patterns weaved themselves along Maplewood panels. An ancient stone arch welcomed guests as they stepped along the battered stone walkway towards the front door. Exotic plants blossomed colorfully along the path.

Jenna felt dwarfed standing in front of the dark wooden entry door. She smiled as she reached for the brass knocker in the shape of a lion's head.

"What are you grinning about?" Halle asked.

Jenna pointed to the lion. "Doesn't it kind of make you feel like you might be visited by the ghost of Halloween's past?" Her eyes widened in a way that was more Eddie Murphy in the *Haunted Mansion* than spooky like Jenna meant it.

Halle shook her head at Jenna, but had to admit, it reminded her of the one that adorned Ebenezer Scrooge's door, only a whole lot creepier. It was the perfect setting for anything Halloween related.

Jenna pressed the small glowing button to announce their arrival.

When no one came, Halle reached for the brass lion and slammed it down a few times. The sound echoed, resonating eerily in the rafters of the outdoor stone foyer. A minute later, one of the two mahogany doors creaked opened slowly in classic scary movie fashion. Halle had never been to Levi's house before. She was currently thinking there was a very good reason for that. Something about the place was making her more than uneasy and she hadn't even stepped foot inside yet. The senses she had been contending with for the past week weren't helping. They hadn't retreated to their rightful place at the return of her sight. Every sound, scent, touch was still amplified.

Jenna stepped through the entrance ahead of Halle, following the butler who had opened the door and leading the way down the corridors toward the sound of music echoing from the twelve foot ceilings. It was classic movie scene décor. The interior of the house resembled a castle straight out of an English history book. Neat rows of suits of armor and dark tapestries served as testaments to an ancient time lining the long hallway that led to the large open room at the end where people were already gathered. Asa had gone all out to recreate a time gone by. There wasn't an electric light to be seen. The length of the corridor and "ballroom," as the butler referred to it, was lit entirely by candlelight. It was an amazing display.

"It looks so much like..." Jenna spoke so softly Halle almost didn't make out what she said. It had blended in with so many other voices.

"Like what?" she asked Jenna.

"Nothing. It's just incredible."

They entered into the ballroom, strolling past a group of classical musicians who had taken up residence to one side of the space. Rich, entrancing tones flowed around the room so fluidly and boldly that Halle was certain the room had been acoustically designed for such instruments to be played there. It was beautiful how they had taken modern music and adapted it to classical instruments. Couples were already dancing in the glow of the candlelit room, a light that made it even more difficult to recognize the faces behind the masks.

Halle had chosen one that feathered out over her cheeks and face specifically to make herself less recognizable. An effort that didn't matter it seemed. Matt quickly found them, no doubt because Jenna had described in great detail their dresses to him on more than one occasion.

"You going to be okay, Hal?" Jenna asked as Matt held his hand out.

"Of course. Go. Dance. Be merry...or scary...or whatever." Halle smiled as Matt whisked Jenna off to the dance floor.

Grazing the edges of the room to try to keep out of the crowd, Halle took in the beauty of the hand carved wood and floor to ceiling bookshelves. It was a hauntingly beautiful place. She wondered if it had the same effect when lit by electricity.

Moving further away from the clumps of people, she attempted to block out the voices with little success. She was no longer certain if the voices she was hearing were untethered to bodies or if her newly acquired super hearing simply had her hearing every conversation within a quarter-mile radius. It felt like a bit more than she wanted to handle. When she saw the less populated room toward the back of the home that looked out over Lake Arella, she gravitated toward what she hoped was a quieter setting. She stopped by a set of oversized windows that spanned from floor to ceiling and opened up to a view of rolling hills beyond the lake. The view was breathtaking, a nearly full moon casting its glow across the lake, making a path toward her.

He saw her there, framed by the wall of glass and a moon that seemed to create a glow around her. She stood with her back to the crowded room. The crimson red of her dress pulling at his attention, the ribbon that laced delicately up her bare back brought a smile to his lips. Her presence drew him to her, like so many times before. He reached his hand out and gently touched her shoulder, sending an arctic shiver through every cell of Halle's body, almost causing her to drop the fan Jenna had insisted she carry.

"Leah?" The icy voice was razor sharp but deeply masculine.

She turned to face him, startled. "I'm sorry. I'm not Leah." Something about him felt oddly familiar. The mask covered his face, but his eyes, every aspect of his glare held a hypnotic attribute. One that Halle was almost certain she'd been exposed to before. A knot formed deep in her core, bringing with it a nauseous quality.

When he spoke again, his voice spilled out like sweet poison, deadly but captivating at the same time. "I'm sorry. You look very much like her, and...your dress. May I ask where you got it?"

Halle was distracted for a moment by the scent of cigars and burnt meat. She looked toward what she thought was the kitchen. The caterers would likely hear about this. From what Halle had heard about Asa, he was very particular. Her attention came back around to the elegant man, who clearly had to be one of Asa's friends. He appeared to be mid-twenties, well built and very comfortable in a tailored suit. Something that gave him a different air than most of the high school and college students attending the party.

"It was my grandmother's actually. Family heirloom."

"You're grandmother has exquisite taste. I knew a woman once, in Ireland, who had a dress very much like this one. Though I'm certain the dress is only embellished by the beauty wearing it."

"Thank you. That's interesting. My grandmother lives in Ireland." She tried to focus on the music to drown out the voices. Still with little success.

"Your necklace, was that your grandmother's as well?"

Halle lifted a hand to caress the black satin ribbon that held the cross she had discovered in the base of the angel, the gift her father had left for her. "No. My father gave it to me."

"It's really quite intriguing. I am a bit of an antique connoisseur, do you know its origins?"

"No, my father died when I was very young."

"Did you say your grandmother is from Ireland?"

"Yes." Voices rattled in her head. She tried to focus on what the man before her was saying, but there were so many voices vying for her attention.

"Where are my manners? Please, allow me to introduce myself?" He reached out a hand.

Mindlessly she held out her hand in reaction to his gesture, intent on merely shaking his hand, instead he brought it to his lips.

"My name is Apollo. It's a pleasure to meet you, Miss?"

"Michaels." It slipped quietly from her lips as she focused on the voice breaking through all the noise. Standing out from every other voice in her head. Every other one seemed to fade and there it was. Calling her name.

Halle.

She recognized his faint Australian lilt.

"I'm so sorry," she said, glancing over his shoulder. "Would you excuse me?" It was said as she tried to smile politely and slipped her hand from his, then turned to walk toward the voice that had shattered the white noise.

Halle. Where are you?

She scanned the crowd. How would she recognize him behind the mask? She knew the voice. Would know it anywhere. Her name sounded so different spilling from his tongue, beckoning her like a homing device. How could she hear him so clearly through all the background noise? Through all the voices that had been so difficult to shake free of only moments before? The questioned played through her mind even though she knew if she called out to him, he wouldn't hear her.

Aedan. Where are you? She thought it for the third time.

Halle, turn around.

She stopped, complying as though he had been standing right behind her, speaking over her shoulder. Slowly, she twirled around, scanning the smiling faces as she moved, fixing her eyes across the room, and locking with his gaze the moment they connected. The immediate link drew him to her.

As if motivated by an uncontrollable gravity, they both began making their way through the crowd. Stares still connected as they weaved through the masses, stopping only when they stood face to face, their bodies nearly joined. Neither of them said a word. Aedan held his hand out and she placed hers in his palm as he slid the other to her waist, wrapping it around her, pulling her closer and holding her protectively. With a tilt of her head, she looked up at him. Even behind the mask, his eyes shimmered like moonlight on the sea; bore into her soul, just like in her dreams.

After several minutes, Halle broke the silence between them.

"I need to tell you something."

His chest rose sharply with his breath, a slow nod encouraged her to speak.

"You might think I'm crazy, but . . ." she hesitated, realizing at that moment that every other voice was gone. In that moment, it was just the two of them.

"Halle, you can tell me anything."

Her voice quivered, uncertain if she wanted to share her secret with this man she barely knew. "My dreams. They. I." She hesitated.

As though he could read her thoughts, he smiled softly down at her and spoke. "Your secrets will always be safe with me, Halle." The faintest hint of his accent traced his words.

"I don't dream like everyone else. I dream about places I shouldn't know. Things I shouldn't know. I dream about you. In fact, I have dreamt about this exact moment." She searched his eyes, aching for something that would assure her he wasn't going to disappear like he always had in her dreams. "Only, you always leave."

His gaze sought to understand what was driving her to open up. "Why are you telling me this?"

"Aedan, I dreamt about you long before I actually knew you. It scares me, but at the same time, it makes me feel like I've known you forever. Like I could trust you with my life, with everything I hold closest to me. You are nothing like anyone I've ever known and, yet . . . I keep expecting you to leave. Like in the dreams. Like my dad left. Like Cam left. People leave. They always leave."

In that instant, he knew there couldn't possibly be an ounce of malice in Halle Michaels. No matter what Bastian or Osiris said. No matter what his orders, he had to protect her. Even if it meant protecting her from himself. His hand slipped behind her neck as she spoke, her eyes fighting back tears. His fingers laced in her hair and he steadied his eyes with the blue-green gaze looking back at him. Slowly, he brought his forehead to rest softly against hers.

"Then I guess it's a good thing I'm not like people." She could never be left as a casualty of battle. As long as he had breath, she never would be.

"I need to tell you something too, but not here. Somewhere we can have a little more privacy." He kissed her forehead and took her hand, leading away from the crowd.

Jenna caught her arm just as they were about to leave the ballroom.

"Hal, I have to talk to you a minute." She glanced to the towering Adonis holding Halle's hand. "Aedan. How are you?" Her tone dripped with aloofness.

Aedan glanced back at Halle. "Never better, Jenna. And yourself?"

"Peachy. But I just need to borrow Halle for one minute. Okay? Promise I'll send her right back."

Aedan and Halle exchanged an unspoken agreement as Jenna dragged Halle through an archway beyond the musicians and into the library.

"What are you doing?" Jenna's tone was one of an interrogator, not a best friend at this point.

"I was dancing and talking." Halle eyes Jenna curiously.

"I saw him kiss your forehead, what was that about?"

"Your guess is as good as mine, but I was about to find out before you so rudely interrupted." Halle grinned at Jenna, whose stern expression didn't change. "Okay Jen, spill it. What do you have against Aedan? Has he done something I don't know about?"

Jenna took a deep breath. "Halle, I just don't think he's who you think he is. I don't want you to get hurt. Again."

She smiled softly at her best friend. "Thank you. I love you for that. I do. And I appreciate that you're concerned, but I'll be fine. Really. Besides, someone told me I need to step out of my comfort zone. Follow my dreams. He's in there. Consider this, me following my dream. Literally."

Halle smiled at her best friend and glided off into the hallway.

Twenty minutes later a firm hand wrapped around Jenna's arm.

"Where's Halle?" Aedan had been looking for her for ten minutes unsuccessfully.

"She went to find you, but that was twenty minutes ago. Easily."

"Clearly, she didn't find me." Aedan gave a stern, worried look.

Panic filled Jenna's eyes. "We have to find her. She can't be that hard to spot, deep red dress. Kind of stands out."

"Yeah, and she glows," he mumbled.

"What did you say?" A puzzled glare stared back at him.

"Nothing."

"You said she glows. Crap. If you see it that means . . ." Jenna took off through the crowd of ball gowns and tuxedoes.

Aedan hesitated, trying to grasp what Jenna meant. He quickly caught up and stayed close behind her as she maneuvered through the sea of people.

"What do you mean if I see it? Jenna!" He shouted over the music.

She kept moving, sweeping from one room to another.

"You know what this house is, don't you?" He demanded. Waiting for her to respond.

She didn't answer, he opened a link with Jess.

"She's gone, Jess. If you're not cloaked, get that way. Now. And search this entire house. Every closet, every corner. If she's here. Find her."

"I'm on it."

Aedan found Jenna outside, eyes closed, like she was worried and thinking intently, unless she was searching for something. But that would mean that Aedan suddenly understood so much about the spunky platinum blonde. The question was, was he right?

"What are you looking for Jenna? Or do you prefer your given name?"

She opened her eyes and cut him a glare that possibly might have killed in the past. "Now is not the time to hash that out Aedan. We have to find her. You know that. If Apollo gets to her first."

"I'm not so sure Apollo is the worst of it."

Jenna tilted her head and raised an eyebrow, listening. Waiting for him to continue.

"I think it's possible someone on our side is after that book and they don't care who they have to stab in the back to get it."

"Who? Have you talked to Darius about this?"

"I don't think we can go to Darius. It's not safe. I'm afraid this is up to me, you, and Jess."

"Did someone call my name?" Jess appeared out of thin air. Uncloaked. "She's not here. I checked everywhere. No sign of her."

"I wouldn't say that." Jenna moved slowly toward the driveway. She knelt down and picked up the black lace fan she had insisted Halle carry with her. "This is definitely a sign, just not a good one."

"Hey, Jenna, there you are." Matt emerged from the house. "Hey Aedan, and whoever you are." Matt stuck his hand out to Jess. "Hey, I'm Matt."

Aedan cocked his head, unaware that Jess could take physical form. He'd just assumed only he and Jenna were aware of his presence.

Jess shook Matt's hand. "Jess. I'm a friend of Aedan's. Nice to meet you."

"Have you guys seen Halle? I heard Brandt was looking for her, and I was going to try to make sure Aedan shut that down." Matt grinned.

Jenna shot Aedan a look before focusing on Matt, changing her demeanor back to bubbly Jenna. "I think she wasn't feeling well. I'm going to go check on her. Would you get me something to drink while I do and I'll meet you on the patio?"

"Will do. Aedan, I'll see ya later. Jess, it was nice to meet you." Matt turned to leave.

When he was back inside, Jenna took a breath. "Okay, I'm going to handle Matt and the story about why Halle and I are leaving. You two...just find her. I'll catch up with you."

Chapter Eighteen

Halle opened her eyes to find herself surrounded by utter darkness. The first thought to race through her mind was that her sight was gone. Again. She tried to turn her head to look for a light, but she couldn't move. There wasn't enough room. Her muscles locked into place in the tight space.

She tried to remember. Aedan. The dance. Jenna. Then came the warning as she searched the crowd again for Aedan. And the mysterious party-goer who had told her a tall, well-built guy was looking for her outside. The last thing she could remember was talking to Brandt – who happened to be the guy who had been looking for her – and him going inside to get her a drink. Then a rustling sound accompanied by a shadow moving faster than humanly possible and the smell of paint thinner? Ending here – in a small dark space.

Why did these things keep happening? Was she suddenly a magnet for all things worthy of their own Paranormal Activity episode?

Okay, get it together Halle.

She closed her eyes tight and tried to focus her senses. Cigars. Maybe she was still at Levi's house. And something else. Mint. She pushed the smells aside to concentrate on the sounds. Watching so many episodes of *Psych* was suddenly coming in handy. Pay attention to what you hear in your surroundings. A door, large, wooden, very heavy. Possibly still at Levi's. That's when the faint sound slammed against her senses, the bell. From her dream. It was the same bell. Her skin crawled at the thought. Something had been chasing her in that dream. She needed to get out of wherever she was. She needed to get away.

Voices grew closer. *Play dead or at least unconscious, Halle. Element of surprise.*

"I won't allow you to dispose of her." She knew that voice. It was the poisonously sweet tone from earlier.

"You surprise me, Apollo. You've never been one to be protective. Of anything, much less anyone." A female voice. Vaguely familiar.

"This one belongs to me. You seemed to

know that before I did. I'm sure you can see my reasons for not permitting you to destroy something that is mine."

A soft chuckle, full of amusement. "She is your problem. As long as we get what we need, do as you wish with her." Mint. She was chewing gum. Mint gum.

"Very well. Let's find the book so that you can be on your way." Apollo's footsteps grew heavy and close.

He stopped just short of Halle's location. Raised a hand to his head.

"Is there a problem, Apollo?"

There was something in the female voice that made Halle question her intentions. The timbre of her tone was icy and dangerous, as though she would just as soon strike Apollo down as speak to him.

Apollo stood dead still for a moment, held his hand up to the woman next to him and closed his eyes, shaking his head slightly. Like he was trying to rid himself of a thought. He couldn't believe what he was hearing. Shocked that any Guardian had the ability to open a mental link to him.

"Apollo, if you can hear me, I have something you might want. One minute, meet me on the neutral corner by the Safe House. Alone."

He didn't have time to respond. The link

was gone as quickly as it was opened.

"Zadok." Apollo called the shadow demon to him. "Guard her. If she takes even a step toward the girl, slice her in two." Zadok nodded. "I shall return in a moment." He turned to the exotic woman standing by. "Please excuse me."

Aedan was waiting for Apollo when he arrived.

"Aedan. It's been too long. That was quite the neat little trick you pulled there."

"Where is she?"

"I'm afraid you're going to have to be a tad more specific. You see, I have had a number of shes recently."

Aedan took a few steps closer. "Halle. Where. Is. She? I won't ask nicely again."

"I'm not sure who this Halle is, Aedan. And you should really work on your 'nicely.' Now, I don't mean to be rude, but I do have company waiting."

Aedan felt a parade of emotions run him over as he stepped nose to nose with Apollo.

"Let me make myself crystal clear." Aedan spoke softly but there was a dangerous edge to his voice. His fists clenched, loosened, and clenched again as he spoke.

"If you kill her, if you hurt her in any way, if she slips and falls and needs a bandage on her skinned elbow, if she has one tiny scratch, one hair out of place, I will spend eternity making you pray for mercy that you know will never come, and when I'm done...you'll be alive. You'll wish you weren't, but you'll have no way to scream in pain. No way to end your own miserable existence. Eternity, Apollo. And we both know just how long eternity can be for us."

"Oh, Aedan. I do believe you have a soft spot for this girl. You know how dangerous soft spots can be. But don't you worry; if I happen to come across her, I'll be sure to send her your love. Now, I really must be going. Company awaits. Please, do keep in touch." He traced before Aedan could respond, but not before Jenna got a bead on his pattern.

Jenna's voice rang loud and clear through Aedan's head. *"Grrrrrr!!! He's a little craftier than I gave him credit for."*

"Still nothing?"

"No. David Copperfield hit up over a dozen places before tracing to the one he wanted to end

up at. I have to give him props. That was smart."

"Well, there is likely a good reason he's third on the food chain." Jess joined in on the conversation.

"Okay, we are going to have to think. What are the odds he knows what we know?" Aedan wasn't sure of what exactly Jenna knew.

"Crap."

"What is it now potty mouth?" Jess was already ribbing Jenna.

"I gave Darius a copy of the phrases Halle and I had untangled from the journal. Which means, they were probably passed along to Bastian and Osiris."

"Okay, everyone, Halle's room. Now." Aedan arrived first.

"We need that list, Jenna." Aedan was already beginning to grow impatient. The longer Apollo had Halle, the less he liked it. Aedan had seen what Apollo did with his playthings.

Jenna fumbled through some things on Halle's desk. "Here. Got it."

"The book. Do you know where that is? We might need it." Aedan's tone was pure business.

Jenna pointed to the bed. "It's under there. Jess, be a dear and grab it, would you?"

"As you wish, milady."

Once Jess had the book and Jenna had the

paper, the one and only thing Aedan knew to do was find some leverage.

Chapter Nineteen

Halle waited for the footsteps to fall close by her dark prison and she closed her eyes. Made herself seem as unresponsive as possible. When the trunk opened, Apollo reached in and cradled her gently from the space. Her body limp in his arms. She had no idea what it was they wanted from her – she didn't care. It couldn't be good and whatever it was, she had no intentions of giving it to them.

"Do you have the second book?" Apollo's voice oozed, she wanted to hurl. Nausea was tight in her stomach. That seemed to be a pattern being near him.

"We were unable to get it, but we do have the inscriptions found in it. I don't know what makes you think this mortal can decipher it when we could not." Her voice was cold and filled with disdain. She clearly held a grudge against mortals. Or at least against Halle. Wait. Mortal? Halle processed the possibilities. *No.* She had to be dreaming this. Her mind raced, trying to consider the possibilities. Her father's words suddenly resonated.

Apollo scoffed at the blonde's condescending attitude. "You know for yourself, she is no mere mortal. If you recall, she belongs to me. Do not underestimate her, as you clearly have all this time." He walked as they spoke, but the movements weren't jarring, they were smooth. Almost like floating.

"Well then, wake her or I shall do it my way. We need to find this book and be done. I am growing bored of it all."

"Now now, Niki. You cannot rush success." Apollo placed Halle in a chair. A hard, stone chair. "Halle, Halle my dear. We need your help with something." He swiped something under her nose briefly. She flew up, gasping for air.

"Oh my great, what was that?" Her sense of smell felt like it tripled whatever the scent was. Regardless it was pungent and more than she could stand.

"My apologies, Halle. Do you remember me? We met earlier at the party." He sat in what appeared to be a stone pew behind her.

"What's going on? Why am I here?"

Apollo leaned forward, resting his arms on the back of the pew Halle sat in and studying her face closely, her mask from the ball now gone. "We need your help, Halle." He smiled a cold smile. "Your father left a book behind and we need to find it."

"My father? I was a year old when he died. I don't know anything about my father or any books he might have had."

"Well, my dear, we think you might. Even if you don't know that you do."

"We don't' have time for thi —"

Apollo held one finger up to shush the radiant blonde whose skin spoke of a far off land.

"Halle, it's kind of important that we find this book. The fate of the world as you know it could very well depend on it."

Halle tried to process. Things were not making sense. Even for her dreams. But this was not a dream. She wanted to tell herself it was, but she knew better. There was a characteristic to her dreams that was recognizable. It was not here. She glared at the elegant man with poison words. He was beautiful. Much like . . . No.

"Well this night is just going to hell in a hand basket fast." She mumbled under her breath, staring at the sharp lines of his jaw, the pallid color of his skin. When she met the piercing green eyes it startled her, but she made sure not to show it.

Apollo laughed. It was the laugh of a madman laced in charm.

Her father's words came rushing in. *"Things are changing for you, Halle. There are a lot of things out there Halle, things you don't understand. Things you aren't aware of. Things that can hurt you...and your mother."*

"How did you know my father?" Her stare bore into him. She needed to buy some time, time to figure out what she could do to escape.

He studied her, her features, her poise. How she held herself upright and leaned forward, a show of aggression in the face of what she surely must consider as danger. She was afraid, he knew she was, he could sense it. Yet, she did not show it by any human indications.

"Interesting." A slow, shadowy smile threaded his lips.

"Apollo, we do not have time for this little game of catch-up. We need to get to work. You can discuss bonding with your pet later." Nakita was irritated. "I have to answer back, and the longer this takes, the less likely you are to get what you want from this."

Apollo appeared annoyed at being giving a time frame. He cut his eyes briefly at Nakita. Halle guessed he wasn't used to having anyone else tell him what to do. "Very well. Give me the list." He held his hand out without looking at her, his gaze still on Halle, waiting until Nakita placed the paper in his palm.

"I am going to keep an eye on the perimeter." She glared at Apollo as she left. Halle sensed there was an unspoken conversation between the stares.

"Halle, my dear, what can you tell me about this?" He handed her a copy of the email translations Uncle T had sent her. Complete with Jenna's scribbles of verses and numbers.

"Where did you get this?" Halle glared at him, suddenly aware of all the times she had felt she was being watched or followed. Aware of all the moments in her life that she knew she wasn't alone, even in an empty room.

"That doesn't really matter at the moment, does it dear?" He may have looked as though he blended perfectly into the twenty-first century, but something in his words spoke of a more ancient time. Something in his demeanor exuded a sense of propriety and charm lacking in the world.

A charm she knew was nothing more than a façade. This man would destroy anything in his path to get what he wanted. That wasn't a question in her mind. Halle silently prayed Lana was safe. She wouldn't dare ask aloud. No way was she giving ideas that might not have occurred to him. She looked at the paper in his hand again.

"It's mine. It's just something I scribbled from some Latin phrases I came across. Why? And why do you have it?" She maintained a hard glare, trying not to break eye contact. "It is nothing relating to my dad, I know that much."

His shadowy smile widened, appearing delighted. "Such composure."

"Who are you?" Halle asked, almost defiantly.

"I did introduce myself earlier, only you were pulled away by something. Or was it someone?"

"I know your name," she spoke through tight lips. "I want to know *who* you are."

His eyes held what Halle almost recognized as pride. "I am here to help, Halle. I've always been here." He paused and took a noticeable breath, considering that she would be more cooperative if she had answers.

"I know that you believe in God, Halle. Don't you?"

She nodded.

"I have stood in His throne room. I have watched over His creations since the dawn of time. Your father, he was one of God's chosen and this book we seek, it holds secrets that need to remain that way. Secrets your father was entrusted with. Secrets your father gave his life for."

Halle glared at him. She saw there was truth in his eyes, but it was mixed with something else. Evil. Truth mixed with lies. Could he read her as easily? Is this what her father meant? *"You need protection from me and everything that I have inadvertently brought to your doorstep."* Is this what he brought to the doorstep? Protection. Aedan. His image flashed through her mind. He couldn't protect her from this. There was no protection from this. Just like every other fear she had faced in her life. She was on her own.

"I'm not so sure I believe you." Halle prayed her voice sounded stronger than she felt on the inside. "You say you have stood in God's throne room. How do I know you aren't just some madman who thinks you are an angel of God or something? Some twisted individual with an agenda who thinks I'm something I'm not?"

He broke into laughter that sounded nothing less than cruel on Halle's ears. To anyone else it would have been a jovial laugh, but she heard so much more entwined between the tones. "Angel? There's one I haven't heard in a while. Warrior would be a more appropriate term, my dear." He held a hand out as though he cupped a bowl in it and a red light began to fill it. It reminded

her of the electricity globe at the science museum.
The one that sparked to the touch when you placed
your hand on the glass. Only this looked and felt
much more dangerous. Its energy reached out
toward her, inviting her to it. She fought the urge
to reach out and touch it. He sucked it back into his
hand like a vacuum in a blink. Who was this man? If
he was even a man at all.

"Now, about the book." His voice snapped
her from her thoughts. "I need you to help me.
Your paper there. I happen to think you're on to
something."

"Why should I help you?"

He smiled. "That is a valid question. One I
can understand your need for an answer to, but I
don't have time for extensive convincing, Halle.
What is comes down to is this – this book we seek,
your father's book, holds the fate of a million souls
between its pages. You can help save those souls.
Help them find their way home where they truly
belong. Without your help, they are sure to be
damned to an eternity of suffering. They need you,
Halle."

Halle looked at the paper and looked
around. She didn't recognize her surroundings, and
that was an uneasy feeling. The walls appeared to
be made of pure stone. No modern amenities.
Pews carved of wood and stone. A carved wooden
crucifix hung at one end of the room. Nothing

extravagant but still intricate and beautiful even though it was run down.

"Did this used to be a church?" Halle asked as she stood, spinning around to take it all in. A wooden carving of the last supper hung over a door opposite the crucifix.

"It did. It has been somewhat lost with time and clearly neglected. Shame really."

Halle heard the sarcasm creep into his words.

"Why are we here?" She asked as she read over the phrases on the paper again silently, trying to hold them to memory.

"My associate, the overbearing blonde outside, believes your father might have brought the book here. For safe keeping."

Halle glanced around. "Why? This place doesn't appear very safe." Stall. Think of an escape plan. She continued to scan the room. One way out – the front door. Surely Nakita would be there waiting. She had to keep him in the mindset that she was willing to help. That was her only exit strategy. She read over the phrases again.

"At one time, this was the safest place on earth."

"What happened?" She moved closer to the front door. Looking around at the designs, gliding her hands across the cold stone as she walked.

"Time happened." He snapped his head to her, as though he were reading her thoughts.

She stopped at the door and stared at him, then read from the paper.

"Begin here. In the presence of the people, within a place for repentance. At the threshold of the Apostles, lift your faces to the Light." She looked up toward the ceiling, to the round opening above the crucifix. "Would that be the light?" She pointed to it. He turned his head to look at the opening. When he did, she ran.

Chapter Twenty

"She was here." Aedan pulled a small piece of torn red fabric from the rusted iron handrail.

"This is where he brought her? Why?" Jenna scanned the area. "This place hasn't been used in ages."

Jess began walking the perimeter the moment they arrived. "I'm picking up a trail."

"Do you think it's Apollo?" Aedan was at Jess' side before he could blink.

"Not sure, but whoever it was they were moving slowly. So they were either out for a leisurely stroll or looking for something."

"Or someone." A smile formed on Aedan's lips. "You gotta love her."

Jenna knew immediately. Halle wouldn't go

down without a fight.

"So let's go through the scenarios. We know if she did give them the slip, it probably won't be for long. So we have to move fast."

Jenna grinned. "They left a trail. Maybe they didn't think we'd find them. I love it when I'm underestimated."

Jess' smirk turned up one corner of his mouth. "Are you thinking what I'm thinking?"

Aedan's voice was sharp. "If it involves watching Apollo and anyone else responsible for putting Halle in harms' way burn within lux dei, I might be."

Jess gave it a brief thought. "I was thinking element of surprise, but I'm good with you following it up with that."

"The trail is still burning hot. Let's go. I doubt we have a lot of time."

The headstone came out of nowhere. Halle tumbled to the ground, the agony of pain searing through her knee. That was definitely going to leave a bruise, if not worse. How did she not see that? She saw it clearly, lying on the ground beside it. She lay there for a split second, listening to the sounds of the night. Or the lack of. Deathly quiet came to mind. Ironic, in a cemetery. She stood, rubbing her knee and contemplating the best direction to head in.

The moon hid stealthily behind the clouds. She barely had enough light to see ten feet in front of her when her sight had been at a hundred percent. Tonight she was lucky if it were at seventy. After a deep breath to calm herself and gather her bearings, she saw them. The shadows of headstones scattered across the hill. Another dream slapping her in the face. She didn't wait for what she knew was coming. She grabbed the front of her dress, pulling it away from the ground and ran. Praying her vision was accurate enough to dodge the headstones. She knew they were coming for her. Her ears searched the night for the sound of the bell she had heard so clearly in her dream, something inside knew the bell was calling her for a reason. Finally its faint chiming was there in the distance, she honed in on it. Zeroed her senses on its eerie summoning. As it grew louder, she knew she came closer to her only chance at survival. She wrenched her head around time and again, expecting to find her hunters there each time, and continued to run as fast as her legs would take her. Knowing if she stopped, those same legs would threaten to collapse beneath her.

How far could one cemetery stretch

anyway? She rounded the top of another hill to find a familiar and comforting sight. Mt. Sion. Even though it was pitch dark, not a light glimmered from it, it was a beacon. A place she knew. A haven. She ran until the chiming of the bell was all that filled her ears.

She felt safe inside. She had always felt safe inside. Hardly able to force herself to slow down, she ran until she slammed herself against the front door to stop. Locked. Of course it was locked. Immediately her feet moved to the only other entrance on the side. Locked again. The bell chimed. The tower. There was a door that opened into the bell tower. She willed her legs to move until she was collapsing against the doorframe praying as she pressed the latch. It clicked and she all but fell inside, pushing it closed behind her. With her back against the door she slid to the floor. Panting for air. Trying to make sense of the last hour of her life.

She brought her hands to her head and realized she still held the paper tightly gripped between her fingers. The wind howled outside, pushing the bell to chime again. Echoing down into the tower. She prayed it was loud enough to mask her gasps for air.

When the wind died down and the chiming subsided, she heard them.

"Are you sure she came here?" Nakita. She

was close. That meant Apollo.

"I can smell her. She's close." Apollo's footsteps echoed through the ground. Halle felt every step vibrate through her.

She was processing his last comment when the putrid smell of cigars and burnt meat hit her again. He smelled her? Well, she could smell him too. Then the mint. The vibrations grew stronger. Halle held her breath and wanted to kick herself for not checking to see if there had been a way to lock the door from the inside. Not that it would have mattered. Apollo could just take the door out with his red ball of electricity. She didn't even want to think what it would do to flesh.

She closed her eyes and focused her mind on what she knew would calm her, center her. Her heart smiled. She had no idea why he was her calm place, but it worked. She took a slow, deep breath and prayed. It was silent to the world, but deafening in her mind.

Show me what to do. I know you can hear me, God.

Mom. Jenna. Matt. Aedan. I might never see them again if you don't help me.

God, please. Show me what to do.

The scent of cigars and mint grew stronger. They were outside the door. Everything went quiet and his voice sliced through the silence like a knife.

Halle.

She couldn't believe how clearly she could remember the sound of his voice.

Halle, just hold on. I will find you.

Was he close by? Was he calling out to her? Was her hearing that . . . Oh god. If he was that close, he'd be in danger too.

Aedan? No. Stay away. She thought. She wanted to scream it, pray he'd hear her, but she knew she couldn't draw attention to her position. When the voice broke through again, it was different.

Halle? Can you hear me? Confusion hammered through his words.

She said his name in her head again. *Aedan?*

What? He answered back.

How? Okay, you're losing it Halle. Keep it together.

Halle, I hear you. You're not losing it.

How can you hear me? She tried to control her breathing, knowing Apollo was just beyond the door to the bell tower.

I was kind of wondering the same thing. But Halle, it doesn't matter right now, where are you?

B- but.

Later, Halle. Where are you?

In the church tower at Mt. Sion. It's . . .

I know where it is. Are you safe?

She listened for the voices outside the door. They weren't as close as she had previously thought, but they were closer than she wanted.

For now. There's a man, umm, angel, something, I don't know what he is. He formed some crazy scary red fire in his hand. But he's after something my dad has. He thinks I have it or can find it.

Does he know where you are?

I don't know, but he says he can smell me. If he can, it won't take him long to find me.

I'm close. Just hang tight.

He's not alone, Aedan.

I can see that.

The latch on the door above her clicked. She stood quietly and moved to a position in the shadows, behind the door. She felt around, looking for something, anything to use as a weapon. Nothing.

It was him. That much she knew. The door never opened though.

"I wouldn't do that if I were you, Apollo."

His voice rang through the darkness, sounding slightly differently than in her mind only moments before. How did he know this so-called angel? This being that spoke of heaven and mortals. Unless. Halle's hand covered her mouth as realization set in.

"Aedan. You came to visit again so soon. How nice." Apollo stepped away from the door. "Where are my manners? You've met Nakita, haven't you?"

"Niki, I wish I could say I was surprised." Aedan's voice held contempt as he spoke, his glare never swaying from Apollo. He didn't trust him enough to take his eyes off of him.

"Are you going to introduce me to your companions? I know you weren't foolish enough to come alone."

Jess came into view. "Jesshua. I should have expected you, I suppose." Apollo nodded in Jess' direction.

"Leave now, Apollo, and I'll refrain from sending you to what you will wish was your death."

Apollo sneered. "You're here for the girl, aren't you? You don't even care about the book?" His expression was curious. "Do you not know what it leads to? Even Nakita here is aware of its power. Why else would she be willing to sacrifice her soul for it?"

Aedan smiled. "I already have the book."

Shock and disbelief hid itself behind Apollo's cool façade. "And just where did you find it?"

"I don't think that matters."

"Oh, but it does. I won't believe you have it until I see it."

"Very well. Genevieve." Aedan called her name and in a blink she was beside him. Wooden box in hand. She'd been there all along, cloaked. She opened the box to expose the book, smiled snarkily and disappeared again. Putting Apollo and Nakita on guard, wondering not only where she might be, but where she had taken the book.

"I know there are two books, Aedan. Do you think me foolish enough to believe that to be the Book of Dreams?"

"Well, you're foolish enough to associate yourself with her, that's says a lot."

Nakita narrowed her eyes and glared, but never said a word, she rarely had to. Aedan knew she was dangerous.

Apollo turned his head slightly toward Nakita and nodded toward the tower door, without taking his eyes from Aedan.

"Touch her and I will light you up." It wasn't an idle threat. Lux dei was already forming around both of Aedan's hands. "And Nakita, I don't think you want to die tonight. You know how this works."

Nakita already had a hand on the door when Apollo threw the first bolt. He could not call his weapon a light from God. God had no part of him anymore. His was a bolt of pure fire from hell. Infernus. Hellfire. Aedan knew from experience how painful it could be.

Aedan rolled to the side, barely dodging the bolt. Jess moved to attack but was caught unaware by Zadock, who had been hiding in the shadows.

Nakita stormed into the tower. "She's not here!" She yelled to Apollo.

"Find her!" He commanded before hurling another bolt of hellfire.

Chapter Twenty-One

     Halle had no idea where the corridor would take her. It was dark, as dark as the blindness she had just endured for days. A slight breeze flowing through the air chilled her skin, beckoning her to walk in the direction it came from. Maneuvering carefully, she held herself to the walls as she moved, cautious about each footstep. She had only taken a few steps when her mind kicked into gear. How could she not remember that? Her phone. She had tucked it away and tied it tightly in the sheers of the red sash that blended into her dress. A dress that was likely ruined after tonight. She pulled it out and shoved the folded paper from her hand into the sheers for safe keeping. *Please don't be dead.* She pled silently.

The phone lit up beneath her touch. *Thank you, God.* There was no signal, but the flashlight app was about to be put to good use.

The corridor was narrow, but surprisingly free of cobwebs or creepy crawly things.

She stayed close to the wall, regardless of the light now filling the way. It felt safer to have her back guarded, especially in a corridor she was certain held the possibility of surprise. It seemed to go on and on, with several doors not-so-evenly spaced that faded into the darkness beyond her flashlight.

She opened the first one she came to — slowly, cautiously — into a room lit with torches. A room she'd seen before. A large wooden arch built into the wall across the room drew her toward it. She traced her fingers over the carvings. The bell tower on one side, the graveyard on the other. A phrase in Latin beneath. With a curious tilt of her head, Halle pulled the paper back out and unfolded it, scanning the Latin phrases. Vivos voco, mortuos plango. "I call the living. I mourn the dead." The words escaped her lips involuntarily. That's where she had seen the phrase. On the bell. She had climbed the tower once with her Sunday school teacher and class. The inscription was on the bell. All this time, could the phrases have been leading her here? To Mt. Sion? She read the rest of the phrases in the order Jenna had rewritten them. The order the verses could be found in the Bible.

Faith is to believe what you do not see; the reward of this faith is to see what you believe. Begin here. In the presence of the people, within a place for repentance. At the threshold of the Apostles, lift your faces to the Light. The appearances of things are deceptive. From the cross, that which is hidden shall be revealed. The one who dreams holds the key.

"I have to get to the sanctuary." Talking to herself again. Somehow it helped. "Okay. Faith is to believe what you can't see. What I can't see. Geesh. I can see everything right now. Why didn't you tell me this three days ago when I couldn't see anything? Wait. I *can* see everything." She closed her eyes. "See what you believe." She traced her fingers over the carvings again. Slowly, methodically. The carvings weren't just for decoration. They hid a doorway. Her fingertips grazed the center, one groove felt out of place, different. Trusting her instincts, she pushed and opened her eyes as the door opened before her. Stairs.

"Of course there are stairs." She followed them to a door and stopped, her heart racing. Another glance at the paper made her wish Jenna were there to help her interpret. Jenna always helped her focus.

Begin here. In the presence of the people, within a place for repentance. At the threshold of the Apostles, lift your faces to the Light. The appearances of things are deceptive. From the cross, that which is hidden shall be revealed. The one who dreams holds the key.

"The Apostles. Threshold. Okay. I need a threshold." She drew in a calming breath, as calming as she could muster and pressed against the door as easily and quietly as possible, but it was heavy and she leaned against it, not knowing what might wait on the other side. When it was barely open, she stopped and peaked through the crack as much as she could before pushing it completely open. The vestibule. A sigh of relief slipped out and she pushed harder on the door, though it felt more like pushing a wall. She looked back in awe when she stepped through. Maybe because it *was* a wall she was pushing. An entire wall.

Three steps toward the double doors that led into the sanctuary she heard noise beyond the entrance. Light escaped from beneath the entry, another sign of their presence in the sanctuary. Halle froze in place before slowly leaning to peer through the thin strip of glass found on each side of the dividing doors. It couldn't be. What was she doing here? Halle pushed through the doors into the sanctuary.

"Jenna? Why are you...what are you doing here?" She stared at her. Had they taken her too? "You need to get out of here. It isn't safe."

She turned. "I can't do that, Hal." She was holding the wooden box with the journal inside.

"Why do you have that?" Halle eyed Jenna suspiciously. "Why are you here?"

Jenna's eyes pleaded with Halle. "I hope you can forgive me." She placed the box on the back of the piano closest to her.

"For what? Jen —" Halle's stomach turned to knots. Something was terribly wrong here. "Jen, what's going on?"

Jenna took a step toward Halle. "Hal, I need for you to listen to me. I promise I'll explain everything later, but right now...you need to find your dad's journal."

"What is with everybody and the journal?" Her voice held real panic for the first time.

"You need to know something, Hal. You're not crazy. You're not hearing voices, you're hearing conversations. You're dreams, they are real. Most of them. So pay attention to them. They may save your life or someone else's. You've done that already, ya know. Apollo, so not one of the good guys."

"Yeah. I kinda got that vibe."

Jenna smiled. "I kinda thought you would. I knew you'd go down swinging no matter what."

"Jen, just tell me what the hell is going on."

Jenna's smile widened. "That's fairly accurate. Apollo . . . he's a Hellion. Your dad was entrusted with secrets. They are in his journal. We can't let Apollo get them."

"A Hellion? What exactly does that mean?" Halle stared at her best friend, wondering how she was involved in all of this. Wondering if she was even the Jenna she knew at all. So many questions.

Jenna sighed. "He's a demon, Halle. One of the fallen."

Her eyes filled with tears, she fought them back. "Jenna, if he's a Hellion. What are you?"

"I'm your best friend. I'm just not originally from the same neighborhood you are. Look, I really want to explain all of this to you but right now, we're a little pressed for time. Blondie is looking for you. I'm looking for her and you should be looking for the book. Halle, you're the only one who can find it."

"How can you know that? Why only me?"

"Because. The one who dreams, holds the key."

"But I don't wa –"

"Halle! Get down!" Jenna was pushing Halle out of the way one second and lying beside her on the floor the next. Blue fire scorching her shoulder. "Halle, get the book and get it to Aedan. I'm going to take care of Barbie."

In a flash, Jenna had Nakita by the hair and with a ball of light they were gone. Like a miniature supernova. Halle lay there for a moment, stunned.

"Okay, Halle. You can do this. Apparently, you *have* to do this." She stood, pulled the paper open and read. "Apostles, threshold."

After looking around she noticed it. The doorway where the Apostles hung overhead. For the first time she realized they were permanent. No way to ever be moved. Part of the structure. She quickly made her way to the threshold of the doorway and stood.

"Lift your faces to the light. Light? There's light everywhere. Okay, maybe there's too much light." She reached over and flipped the switch by the doorway. The room went dark, with one exception. The crucifix. Bathed in red light, just like every Sunday morning. How? No time for that.

"The appearances of things are deceptive. Hmmph, no kidding. From the cross, that which is hidden shall be revealed." Halle flipped the light back on and ran to the back of the pulpit. Immediately examining the crucifix. It had to be something to do with the cross. Had to. After taking a step back and examining it for a moment, she climbed up onto the chair behind the pulpit, closed her eyes and began to run her fingers over the lines of the crucifix. Nothing. No obvious hidden compartments. What was she missing? *Hidden. That which is hidden*. She examined it again, knowing she *had* to be missing something. Almost by accident she ran her hand behind the base of the cross, between the back panel and the wall. There was a notch. She examined it more closely.

"You have got to be kidding me. The one who dreams, holds the key." She rolled her eyes and reached to remove her necklace. "Really, Dad?" She slid the small metal cross from the ribbon and maneuvered it between the wall and the wood, locking it into place. Nothing happened.

"What am I doing wrong? Think, Halle. Think." She lost her balance a little and tightened her grip on the bottom half of the cross to steady herself. It clicked and the bottom of the wooden crucifix jutted out. "Nice. No such things as coincidence." She pulled the small cross from the groove in the back and held it tightly in her grip while she slid the hidden compartment down to reveal a mass of something wrapped in red velvet cloth. She pulled it out and stepped down from the chair she stood in, peeling back the corners of the red cloth, revealing the book everyone seemed so intent on getting their hands on. This was it. Her father had held this book, written in it, this was what he had given his life for.

"Oh god. Jenna. Aedan." She couldn't allow them to give their lives too. Moments later she was standing in the dark night, listening to the sounds of thunder. Only it wasn't thunder. She knew that. She ran until she found herself standing much too close to the doorway of death.

"Halle!" Her name tore out of him like the thunder that had filled the air. Aedan saw her too late. There wasn't enough time to save her. Zadock wrapped his hand around her throat, pulled the book from her arms and vanished.

In an instant the thunderous roar of battle was gone, there was dead silence. Apollo was gone, Zadock was gone, and Halle's frail form was falling to the earth.

Aedan rushed to her side and fell to his knees, gathering her into his arms. He cradled her lifeless body to his chest. A loud cry rose from his core, alerting Jess and Jenna. He held her to him, rocking her gently as he buried his face in her neck. It couldn't end like this. He couldn't lose her too. It wasn't fair. All of his training, all of the centuries spent protecting humanity and he couldn't keep the one person important to him safe.

When the moist streams stung Aedan's face it took a moment to recognize them for what they were. Tears. His tears. For the first time in his eternal existence, he cried. At that moment he knew this would destroy him. Even losing the child in Egypt hadn't brought him to his knees, hadn't brought him to tears. He had buried that.

"Don't leave me, Halle. Don't do this. I'm not strong enough to exist if I lose you," he whispered, his voice broken, forcing him to choke out his words. "I need you." He angled his head, brushing his lips against her forehead. He kissed her softly, warmly. Honestly enough to reach her soul.

Chapter Twenty-Two

"I don't know how this happened." Aedan sat with his head buried in his hands. "Mortals don't survive the touch of a shadow demon. She never should have been left alone." Aedan looked angrily at Darius as he stood and paced toward the window. "This is their fault – Bastian, Osiris. She shouldn't have been put in the middle of this war."

Darius didn't know what to say. He couldn't explain how or why Halle survived any more than Genevieve could. As a healer, she was more astounded than anyone over Halle's resistance to the shadow demon's touch. She had a theory, but it was only that. A theory.

Darius knew Aedan was right about Bastian and Osiris on a certain level. He also knew that it had been out of his hands. Orders are orders.

Genevieve stepped quietly into the room.

"She wants to see you." She pointed to the Guardian, standing impatiently by the window, staring out at the lake.

Aedan turned and arched an eyebrow. "She's awake?"

Genevieve nodded. "But she's still extremely weak and pretty tired as I'm sure you can imagine. Try not to stay too long. Oh....and she doesn't remember most of what happened. Thought you should know that. So...she doesn't remember what you are Aedan. At least, not for now. I have no idea if or when she'll remember."

Aedan all but ran past her.

Darius laughed. "Do you think we should tell them?"

"Nahh. Let's give her time to remember and come to grips with her new reality before we spring that on her too. Besides, we don't know *what* she might remember and how do you think she'd feel about Aedan – or any of us – if she knew? I think we might want to keep that under wraps for a little bit longer."

"Well, I vote *you* tell her when the time comes." Darius smiled.

"Why me? I'm not that brave." She walked to the couch and sat down.

"You're her best friend. She's less likely to hate you."

"Yeah, the best friend who didn't tell her she was immortal for five years." A snarky smile grew on her lips. "So, what's the word on Nakita?"

"Bastian is being tight-lipped about her punishment. Very under the radar." Darius watched the rain as it began to pelt the window panes.

"I'm not so sure I trust him." She twisted a strand of blonde hair around a finger.

"Aedan feels the same, which is why I am trusting his instincts – and yours – and not telling him we still have the book."

"What do you think Apollo did to Zadock when he found out he had the wrong book?" She laughed. "I would have loved to been cloaked in on that conversation."

Darius laughed. "I'm just glad our Halle is smarter than they gave her credit for. Switching the books was kind of brilliant."

Genevieve grinned. "Never underestimate a woman. Mortal or not."

Aedan pushed the door open slowly and peered in. He smiled at the sight of her resting safely.

"I heard that." She said softly.

"I didn't say anything." He stepped past the door, closing it behind him.

"I heard you smile." She opened her eyes and rolled her head to the side, catching his gaze. The smile spread over his face until it was almost touching the corners of his eyes.

"I can see it's going to be a full time job keeping you out of trouble." He laughed, lacing his fingers with hers as he sat on the side of the bed.

She smirked. "A little trouble isn't always a bad thing. I seem to remember trouble being what brought you into my life."

"I was under the impression you couldn't remember anything."

"I remember enough. I'm sure the rest will come back to me."

Her face brightened, which was all that mattered to him at the moment. She was safe, sound, and somehow alive.

He held on to her hand as though his life depended on it. Maybe it did, maybe she had saved him from the hollow existence he had sentenced himself to. Or maybe she really would be the end of him. Either way, he knew if faced with the choice of following orders or keeping her safe, he'd deny every order to protect her. What she said next made him realize he just might have to make that choice sooner rather than later.

"Aedan, I need your help with something." The way she looked up at him told him this wasn't going to be a run of the mill favor.

"I'll do whatever I can," he responded. "What do you need?"

Her expression went cold, a far-off look he'd never seen from her.

"I don't remember what happened when I left Levi's, but I do know it's something I need to remember. I keep dreaming about a man I met at the party. I keep dreaming that he told me my father's death wasn't an accident." She locked eyes with Aedan. A look that held desperation. "Sapphira told me that your job is classified, but something she said leads me to believe you could help me. Will you?"

She didn't wait for him to respond. "I'm asking for your help, but know this, with or without your support, I will find out who killed my father, and why."

Aedan didn't know what to say. He knew who had killed her father. He also knew the resolve he saw in Halle's eyes. He shook his head, agreeing to help her, knowing what it would mean.

"I'm fairly certain you could be the end of me." He knew she could very easily be both the end of his suffering and the beginning of it.

She smiled. "Sometimes an ending is what you need to create a new beginning."

Appendix

There are many angelic references in the series. Most of my research on the supernatural began with scouring the Bible. If you'd like to see where I obtained my research from, here would be the place to start.

Psalm 91:11 ESV

For he will command his angels concerning you to guard you in all your ways.

Hebrews 13:2 ESV

Do not neglect to show hospitality to strangers, for thereby some have entertained angels unawares.

Jude 1:6 ESV

And the angels who did not stay within their own position of authority, but left their proper dwelling, he has kept in eternal chains under gloomy darkness until the judgment of the great day—

Psalm 34:7 ESV

The angel of the Lord encamps around those who fear him, and delivers them.

Acts 27:23 ESV

For this very night there stood before me an angel of the God to whom I belong and whom I worship,

Matthew 24:31 ESV

And he will send out his angels with a loud trumpet call, and they will gather his elect from the four winds, from one end of heaven to the other.

Revelation 22:6 ESV

And he said to me, "These words are trustworthy and true. And the Lord, the God of the spirits of the prophets, has sent his angel to show his servants what must soon take place."

Matthew 26:53 ESV

Do you think that I cannot appeal to my Father, and he will at once send me more than twelve legions of angels?

Acts 5:19 ESV

But during the night an angel of the Lord opened the prison doors and brought them out,

Exodus 23:20 ESV

"Behold, I send an angel before you to guard you on the way and to bring you to the place that I have prepared.

2 Kings 19:35 ESV

And that night the angel of the Lord went out and struck down 185,000 in the camp of the Assyrians. And when people arose early in the morning, behold, these were all dead bodies.

1 Peter 1:12 ESV

It was revealed to them that they were serving not themselves but you, in the things that have now been announced to you through those who preached the good news to you by the Holy Spirit sent from heaven, things into which angels long to look.

Acts 7:53 ESV

You who received the law as delivered by angels and did not keep it."

John 20:12 ESV

And she saw two angels in white, sitting where the body of Jesus had lain, one at the head and one at the feet.

Genesis 16:7 ESV

The angel of the Lord found her by a spring of water in the wilderness, the spring on the way to Shur.

Hebrews 12:22 ESV

But you have come to Mount Zion and to the city of the living God, the heavenly Jerusalem, and to innumerable angels in festal gathering,

Hebrews 1:7 ESV

Of the angels he says, "He makes his angels winds, and his ministers a flame of fire."

Luke 20:36 ESV

For they cannot die anymore, because they are equal to angels and are sons of God, being sons of the resurrection.

Luke 4:10 ESV

For it is written, "'He will command his angels concerning you, to guard you,'

Luke 1:26-38 ESV

In the sixth month the angel Gabriel was sent from God to a city of Galilee named Nazareth, to a virgin betrothed to a man whose name was Joseph, of the house of David. And the virgin's name was Mary. And he came to her and said, "Greetings, O favored one, the Lord is with you!" But she was greatly troubled at the saying, and tried to discern what sort of greeting this might be. And the angel said to her, "Do not be afraid, Mary, for you have found favor with God.

Mark 1:13 ESV

And he was in the wilderness forty days, being tempted by Satan. And he was with the wild animals, and the angels were ministering to him.

Matthew 2:19 ESV

But when Herod died, behold, an angel of the Lord appeared in a dream to Joseph in Egypt,

Revelation 12:7 ESV

Now war arose in heaven, Michael and his angels fighting against the dragon. And the dragon and his angels fought back,

Matthew 28:3 ESV

His appearance was like lightning, and his clothing white as snow.

Matthew 13:49 ESV

So it will be at the close of the age. The angels will come out and separate the evil from the righteous

2 Samuel 24:16 ESV

And when the angel stretched out his hand toward Jerusalem to destroy it, the Lord relented from the calamity and said to the angel who was working destruction among the people, "It is enough; now stay your hand." And the angel of the Lord was by the threshing floor of Araunah the Jebusite.

1 Thessalonians 4:16 ESV /

For the Lord himself will descend from heaven with a cry of command, with the voice of an archangel, and with the sound of the trumpet of God. And the dead in Christ will rise first.

Ezekiel 28:14-16 ESV

You were an anointed guardian cherub. I placed you; you were on the holy mountain of God; in the midst of the stones of fire you walked. You were blameless in your ways from the day you were created, till unrighteousness was found in you. In the abundance of your trade you were filled with violence in your midst, and you sinned; so I cast you as a profane thing from the mountain of God, and I destroyed you, O guardian cherub, from the midst of the stones of fire.

Exodus 3:2 ESV

And the angel of the Lord appeared to him in a flame of fire out of the midst of a bush. He looked, and behold, the bush was burning, yet it was not consumed.

Psalm 35:6 ESV

Let their way be dark and slippery, with the angel of the Lord pursuing them!

For some very interesting information about how angels and demons co-exist with us, check out this website:

https://bible.org/seriespage/6-survey-bible-doctrine-angels-satan-demons

To learn what the Bible has to say about Dreams and Visions, check out this webpage:

http://www.openbible.info/topics/dreams_and_visions

I found some ridiculously fascinating stuff about Guardians in the Theological Dictionary:

http://www.biblestudytools.com/dictionary/angel/

And if there happens to be a question you have about a particular scene or just something you're curious about...shoot me an email.
You can contact me through the form on my website
www.bridgetteohare.com

Acknowledgments

    There are so many people who have helped me along the way that I really just want to say a BIG thank you to them. My Beta Readers, you guys are awesome and I can't thank you enough for your feedback and time – Gail, Susan, Ryan, and Mark. A special shout out to Mark Hunnemann, thank you so much for your insight into the realm of all things other-worldly.

If you enjoyed **Silent Night**, be sure to check out the third novel in the **Book of Dreams** series, *Dreamwalker.*

ABOUT THE AUTHOR

Bridgette O'Hare is the author of the *Book of Dreams* novel series. A freelance editor, journalist, and traveler who resides in North Carolina with her family, she is also the author of the several ghostwritten novels that she wishes she could publicly claim. To learn more about Bridgette, please visit her on Facebook or at www.bridgetteohare.com.

CPSIA information can be obtained
at www.ICGtesting.com
Printed in the USA
LVHW082027070321
680795LV00052B/865